Mel pointe[illegible]oon. 'And that?' he said.

'Up there.'

'The moon, sir? Now entering her third quarter. High tide is at 0645 hours today, sir.'

'But what's it *for*?'

'I'm sorry, sir, I am not coded with the information you require.'

Mel sat down on the ground and rested his head between his hands.

The first man on the surface of Earth for over 2,000 years, Mel has broken through the Forbidden Levels from those regions deep underground where mankind has eked out its miserable, mole-like existence since the cataclysm which made the surface uninhabitable.

Here is an exciting, inventive novel from a brilliant author whose previous books have been enthusiastically received, two of them – *Breakthrough* and *Phoenix* – choices of the Science Fiction Book Club.

OTHER BOOKS BY RICHARD COWPER

Breakthrough
Phoenix
Domino
*Clone**
*The Twilight of Briareus**
*Worlds Apart**

*Also in Quartet Paperbacks

KULDESAK

RICHARD COWPER

QUARTET BOOKS LONDON

Published by Quartet Books Limited 1973
27 Goodge Street, London W1P 1FD
Reprinted 1976

First published by Victor Gollancz Ltd 1972

ISBN 0 704 31075 9

Printed in Great Britain by
Hunt Barnard Printing Ltd, Aylesbury, Bucks

Knowledge enormous makes a God of me . . .

KEATS, *Hyperion.*

I

From his peep hole above the spring Coney watched the silver bubble drifting down towards the sand-spit which the retreating tide had exposed twenty minutes earlier. His black nose twitched; his round ears flicked back and forth; but never for an instant did he allow his attention to stray. A dry bracken frond rustled faintly and his senses at once recorded "water mouse". A fragrance of sphagnum moss wrinkled his nostrils. A wild bee hummed past a hand-span beyond his whiskers. Two hundred feet below him four pied oyster-catchers were strutting in the ripple at the water's edge. Coney was aware of an almost unbearable tenseness that seemed to be located in the region of his stomach. See: hold: tell.

Ten feet above the drying sand the bubble's gradual descent was arrested. It revolved slowly, one complete turn. 'Amazing', opined the Anthropologist. 'Truly amazing.' Which is to say that the concept of amazement was engendered somewhere within the cortex of the being known to his fellows as "the Anthropologist" and transmitted soundlessly to the corresponding receptive centre in the cortex of his companion "the

Explorer". Both beings had "names" in the terrestrial sense: the Anthropologist's sounded rather like the simultaneous twanging of two adjacent harp strings and the Explorer's resembled nothing so much as the noise of water being poured out of a narrow-necked bottle. Such sounds defy phonetic transcription.

If the human ear might have made a distinction between their names, the human eye, unable to perceive their double hearts and their four vocal chords, would have searched in vain for a distinguishing feature in their forms and faces. Outwardly they were identical twins, and in all but two respects they came as close as it is possible to come to that ideal of godlike physical perfection which was extant among the Ancient Greeks when Praxiteles was in his prime. Their hair was short, fair and closely curled; their noses were straight; their mouths and chins firm; their teeth white and even. They both stood a fraction over six feet in height and, at this particular point of space and time, weighed a trifle over 155 terrestrial pounds. Their limbs were perfectly proportioned and they both possessed the full quota of toes and fingers. Nevertheless, had a human eye been able to range over their naked bodies, it would surely have flickered shyly as it reached the area where the thighs joined the abdomen. At the point where in the human male there droops that Thing of Joy which is a Beauty for ever, these ethereal visitors were as bald and smooth as porcelain. Furthermore their chests carried no such vestigial nipples as adorn the male human breast. In fact, within the terrestrial meaning of the words, it was impossible to say whether they were male or female.

Having completed its turn the bubble recommenced its descent, finally taking up a station about six inches above the damp sand. The two visitors stepped out, or, more precisely, they stepped *through* the translucent membrane of their vehicle which, seemingly ineluctable, appeared to wrap each of them in an all-but-invisible layer of itself before letting them go. As the last umbilical filament detached itself and rejoined the parent capsule, first the Explorer and then the Anthropologist vanished from sight.

From his vantage point above the estuary Coney emitted a sound which was part growl, part whimper. The short reddish brown hair on the back of his neck rose until it was standing perpendicular and his upper lip drew itself back to expose sharp white incisor teeth. He did not know why he growled. Later, perhaps, Mel would be able to tell him. He had seen the silver bubble bulge outwards and then gather itself in again, and some part of him over which he had no control had registered fear. His upper lip quivered and slid tremulously down over his teeth. The bristles along his neck sank slowly back. He wriggled his forepaws into a more comfortable position beneath his jaw and settled down once again. See: hold: tell.

The Explorer and the Anthropologist strolled slowly down the length of the sand-spit. Perceptible only to each other and to those observers whose retinas happened to be sensitive to the infra-red wavelengths, they moved as though over an invisible carpet which cushioned and insulated their tread. They passed within a yard of the shrimp-questing oystercatchers and the birds did not turn a feather. 'Don't tell me—* * * s?' transmitted the Anthropologist and laughed.

The Explorer gave a mental shrug. 'It was bound to happen sooner or later. The carbon-based pattern. . . .'

'But this!' The Anthropologist indicated the sun-dappled hills and the clouds sailing serenely above. 'Who could have believed it?'

'I know what you mean,' agreed the Explorer. 'Why even the salinity conforms to within a tolerance of point five. Roughly speaking it's a mirror image of * * *' (here a mental picture of a familiar, green, cloud-swirled planet passed between them) 'though, of course, the configuration of the major land masses bears only superficial resemblance.'

The Anthropologist frowned. 'And you say you've arrived at a total of * * * ?' (again a concept was exchanged, indicating a time-span in the region of two thousand terrestrial years).

'It's difficult to be specific,' the Explorer explained, 'but the indications point to something around that figure. Our main difficulty has been to trace a progression through the types of artefact.'

'??'

'Well obviously at some point the machines must have become self-perpetuating. Possibly it was a gradual process spread over several generations. We always have to assume the connivance of the inventor race unless we have definite evidence to the contrary.'

'Which you have not found?'

The Explorer shook his head. 'That does not mean that we *won't* find it. After all it was only yesterday that I stumbled on my first irrefutable evidence of racial survival.'

'Which is precisely why I am here.'

'Which is why you are here,' concurred the Explorer.

Over the brow of a hill a mile from where they were standing a silvery, spider-armed, Farming Factor appeared and began spindling busily back and forth among the neat rectangles of ripening cereal. The two visitors watched it for a moment without comment, then the Anthropologist who had, presumably, been following some thought path of his own, enquired: 'I suppose you have considered the possibility of a pandemic?'

'No evidence at all,' replied his companion, 'or, if there was it's been effectively destroyed. Of course you may turn up something.'

'Yes, it's possible, I suppose.' The Anthropologist blanked for a long moment then queried: 'You still haven't told me what brought you here in the first place.'

'Here? Where we are now?'

'No, to this otherwise totally barren and insignificant system. To this particular planet.'

'I followed my * * *.' (The best translation for this is "inner nose".)

'Seriously.'

For answer the Explorer proffered a concept whose nearest terrestrial equivalent would perhaps be the quest for Atlantis or El Dorado, but it was proffered in such a way that the Anthropologist could not be certain whether it was intended humorously.

'I had no idea that you were a * * *.' (No earthly equivalent exists for this, though a skein wound out of the disparate threads of Pantheism, pilgrimage, mysticism and the Hegelian "ineffable synthesis of discordant opposites" might just possibly convey a hint of it.)

The Explorer shrugged, then smiled. 'I admit that I did happen to turn up something curious in the Psychic Archives for this Sector. Did you know that this area was surveyed cursorily in * * * ?' (Here a time-span covering roughly twenty thousand terrestrial years.)

'Of course I knew. What I was hoping to establish was some personal evidence of attempted contact. Obviously not "evidence" within the Codex qualification but—well, you know what I mean.'

The Explorer permitted himself the small luxury of an enigmatic grin but was not, apparently, prepared either to confirm or deny the suggestion.

'It would give me *some*thing to start on,' pleaded the Anthropologist.

'It would be wholly unethical,' chuckled the Explorer.

'So there *was* something. I suspected as much.'

'Intuition. Nothing more. I believe you will find something.'

'Something sophisticated?'

'*Technically* sophisticated by our standards—that I doubt,

or we'd surely have encountered it by now. Culturally or psychically? Well, who knows? There, I've given you all the help I can.'

'Thanks for nothing,' sighed the Anthropologist.

They retraced their steps along the sand bank to where in the mellow glow of the westward-sinking sun the bubble still hovered. When they reached it they turned with one accord and looked back up the estuary. The gawky, metallic Factor, its brief task completed, had vanished whence it had come. The clouds were melting away leaving a vast swathe of pellucid sky. 'Uncanny, isn't it?' mused the Explorer. 'Here particularly.'

'Is that why you brought me here?'

'One of the reasons undoubtedly.'

The Anthropologist nodded. 'If I didn't know, I'd be prepared to swear that * * * lay just around that bend.' (A vivid image of a little lakeside town superimposed upon an aural undertone which recalled a faint, nostalgic carillon of glass bells.)

The Explorer sighed. 'What wouldn't I give to have my fingers round the * * * of my * * * ?' (Concepts untranslatable: boat? flower petal? soaring seagull?)

'Why do we do it?' wondered the Anthropologist.

'Why do * * * s * * * ?' (Again untranslatable. Approximates to "fish/swim: birds/fly: men and women make love.")

Along the slopes of the far inland hills violet shadows were gathering. A solitary star swam up the eastern horizon, a single silvery point of light. The Explorer nodded at it. 'Time for me to be off.'

He stepped back into the bubble and handed out three small bundles. 'Is that everything?'

The Anthropologist nodded. 'I'll be in touch.'

They clasped arms briefly and pressed mouths. 'Don't forget who you are,' chuckled the Explorer.

'My name is "Arfaxis",' replied the Anthropologist in passable English.

'Excellent.'

The Anthropologist stepped back a few paces. The bubble rose, slowly at first, then, gathering speed, dwindled with breathtaking rapidity to a twinkling golden spark which vanished high in the sky overhead.

2

You are aware of pain unlike any you have ever experienced. As you remember what happened you feel your stomach trying to turn itself inside out. So you lie still. You shrink the centre of your body's awareness. You clench tight the breath of your spirit. You try to think of something else—just *something*—anything to take your mind outside your hurt. Think of X3 Australasian hybrid; think of "moon"; think of Ulf Starson; think of—

'*Mel? Mel, are you there?*' The intense, urgent whisper seemed to breathe right into his ear. He heaved himself up, groaning, and felt around cautiously in the total darkness.

'Jo?'

'Oh, *Mel*!' It was thanks for a prayer answered. 'Are you all right?'

Was he? It depended on what you meant by "all right". 'How did you get here, Jo?'

'Seeker followed you then he came and got me. He told that you were asleep. I've got a foodstick for you, Mel.'

'Does anyone know you're here?'

'Only Bitos. Did they hurt you terribly?'

Mel's fingertips roved apprehensively over his naked shoulders, encountered a still sticky weal where the electric lash had flayed off the blistered skin, and gingerly withdrew. Again his stomach heaved. 'Godhole, those shuggers know what they're about,' he muttered. 'I don't think they've salted me, though.'

'Oh, *Mel*!'

He grunted bitterly. 'They said it was to remind me to behave myself. I shan't forget in a hurry.'

There was a faint snuffling sound in the darkness close beside him. A cold, damp nose was pushed against his cheek and then a warm wet tongue was lapping his neck and ear. Mel gathered the soft furry body into his arms and hugged the Partner to him. 'Tell, boy,' he whispered. 'Tell.'

The little animal whimpered excitedly, wriggled up in Mel's arms and pushed his nose against Mel's forehead. At once a jumbled series of vivid pictures flickered into chaotic life in the boy's mind. 'Steady. Steady,' he whispered. 'One at a time now.'

From some concealed niche he was looking down at two Security Handlers. He watched them load his naked, unconscious body on to a floater, fling his clothes on top, then guide it along the tunnel beneath him and out of sight round a bend. A moment of darkness followed, broken by brief flashes of light and then by a small circle of illumination that grew rapidly larger. Next moment he was again peering down into the tunnel and the two Handlers were pacing stolidly towards him, passing below him, and moving away down a long incline. 'The Middle Tracks,' he muttered.

The picture suddenly vanished, was replaced by a flying closeup image of a white ceramic wall and then an oddly elongated perspective of a tunnel down which the distant Handlers were still proceeding. 'Clever old Seeker,' he murmured. 'I wonder if the Godeyes saw that.'

For answer the picture suddenly tilted upwards and immediately overhead Mel saw that the Eye for that particular section of the tunnel had gone blind. Luck? Or had Seeker known? 'Wait, boy,' he whispered. 'Jo, did you come by the Middle Tracks?'

'No, through the Deads.'

'Where are we then?'

'Low Fringes.'

'Aren't the sensors working here?'

'Seeker tells not. He tells the whole of this part dark.'

'Are you *sure*? How did the Handlers get me here?'

'Perhaps they didn't.'

'Well, *something* did.'

'Do you want this food, Mel?'

'What is it?'

'Papple. It's all there was.'

Mel groaned disgustedly, then, still cradling Seeker in his arms, he rose unsteadily to his feet and shuffled in the direction from which his sister's voice was coming.

'Over here, Mel.'

Mel stooped, set the Partner down on the floor then stretched out his hand hesitantly. Three paces more. His fingers brushed the cold metal of the cell door, moved upwards and found Jo's warm fingers crooked round the bars of the grille. He pushed his hand through and touched her face. 'How did Seeker get in?' he whispered.

'Through the vent, I think. Here.'

The plastic tube of food was pushed into his hand.

'I've got something for your back too, Mel. Turn round and I'll try and put it on.'

'What is it?'

'Cure. Mark gave it to me.'

Mel grunted, bit off the end of the foodstick and chewed it moodily. Then he squeezed out a lump, bent down, called Seeker to him and gave it to him.

'Shall I do your back, Mel?'

'All right,' he said. 'I don't suppose it'll make any difference now.'

'What do you mean?'

'Well, the Elds know I was whipped, don't they?'

'Of course they do.'

'But if I'm healed up. . . . Bitos said they count our scars or something.'

'Cure isn't *that* good.'

'How do you know? What about Rill's leg?'

'That's different. Come on, Mel. Turn round.'

Rather doubtfully Mel turned and then backed until he felt the chill of the metal door against his naked buttocks. He shivered. 'Get on with it, Jo. My chub's freezing off.'

Jo reached through the grille and, as gently as she could contrive in the pitch darkness, smeared the salve over her brother's back and shoulders. 'How long will they keep you here, Mel?'

'How do I know?'

'Didn't they tell you?'

'Not a word. *Owch!*'

'I'm sorry,' she said. 'I can't reach down any further. You'll have to do the rest yourself.'

Mel grunted.

'Does it feel any better?'

'A bit,' he admitted. 'Thanks anyway. Now you'd better get back before they come looking for you.'

Jo lingered. 'How far *did* you get, Mel?'

'To that place Coney told. Godhole, Jo, it was *fantastic*!'

'What like?'

'There was silver water there for *miles*. And the roof was all sparks. And, Jo, there was this voice—'

Jo, long since familiar with her brother's imaginative flights, was unable to restrain a burp of disbelief.

'Jo, I swear before the Godeyes I'm not making it up!'

'It sounds a bit like old Negus to me!'

'Ah, shug,' he muttered disgustedly. 'You wouldn't believe it even if I showed it to you.'

'Don't be like that, Mel. It's just that . . . well, it sounds *so* impossible. I mean there can't *be* miles of water. There just *can't*.'

'Well there are,' said Mel sullenly. 'I've seen them.'

'How do you know it was water, Mel? Did you touch it?'

Mel remained wrathfully silent.

Jo waited hopefully for a while then asked humbly: 'Did you manage to bring anything?'

'How could I if the place wasn't there?'

'Did you, Mel?' she persisted.

He relented. 'Maybe.'

'Where is it?'

'I hid it in the Deads.'

'What is it, Mel? Another dream?'

'No. Something weird. I don't know.' He was silent for a moment then asked: 'How's Dog?'

'He's all right. I left him in the van.'

'Is Coney there too?'

'No, he's been gone since firstfood.'

'For you?'

'For *me*? *Coney?* What do you think?'

'Well, who for then?'

'For himself of course.'

Wincing at the pain in his back Mel knelt on the cell floor and called the Partner to him. He felt the little furry body wriggling ecstatically at the unexpected summons, and wondered if he could get Seeker to tell him what he wanted to know. That was the trouble with the Partners, even the best of them often bit off the wrong end of the foodstick. It wasn't that they weren't willing, but that they were *too* willing; they tended to upend their holds and bury you under a vanload of rubbish. Still Seeker was as good as they came. It was worth a try. He scooped the Partner up into his arms. 'Coney?' he whispered. 'Where's Coney gone?'

To his astonishment he felt Seeker tremble violently all over. Then the little creature's muzzle was thrust precipitately into his eye. He had a blurred glimpse of a Partner's hind-quarters and scut disappearing down a ventshaft with totally undignified haste and that was that.

Mel ran his hand in a soothing caress over Seeker's head and rubbed the bases of his ears. The trembling subsided. 'What's going between him and Coney, Jo?'

'I believe Coney jumped Shrub when Seeker was out in the Low Levels.'

Mel grinned. 'Poor old Seeker,' he murmured sympathetically. 'Did you chew his pair off, boy?'

Seeker made a noise that might well have been a mixture of a growl and a chuckle. Mel felt round on the floor, found the foodstick and squeezed off another lump which he gave to the Partner. 'When Coney gets back, see if you can't get him to come up here, Jo. It's important.'

'All right. I'll try. But you know what he's like. He's his own Godhole is Coney.'

'He'll end up processed for sure,' grunted Mel, adding the sombre afterthought: 'If he hasn't already.'

'He's too clever for that, Mel. Much cleverer than old Seeker, really. I wish he *would* breed.'

Mel shivered, just as he had the moment before the whips of the Punishment Factors had crashed across his back. 'You'd better get back, Jo. Call Seeker.'

Obediently Jo pursed her lips and made a soft whickering call. With a brief scrabbling noise the Partner was gone. Swearing softly to himself Mel felt round for the tube of cure and, having found it, began clumsily to anoint those parts that his sister had been unable to reach.

3

Coney eased himself out of the lair and peered cautiously around him. Satisfied that he was unobserved he padded silently down to the spring and lapped thirstily. The water tasted different from the pool in the warrens—not better or worse, just different. He sniffed experimentally at the sphagnum moss and wondered if he could eat it. His stomach rumbled windily and he was assailed by a poignant vision of the foodstalls. On an impulse he bit off a shred of the moss, chewed it briefly and spat it out. Then in a series of rippling hops he regained the ledge from which he had watched so diligently for so long.

The sky to the west was a flaming glow streaked with shreds of purple cloud. High above his head the silver star that had beckoned the Explorer sailed on in benign splendour. Coney sniffed the warm, scented breeze and was about to turn and head for home when something held him. He sniffed again, pointing his nose this way and that, questing for the origin. Man! Yet not man. Like man but not man. Not Mel, and yet who except Mel had ever followed him to the Outside? The aberrant gene that had made Coney into Coney and not into Seeker or Trig dictated now that he remained sifting the languishing air, afraid and curious, and just more curious than afraid. But the scent ebbed and did not come again. Coney waited a little while longer and then turned away.

He moved in the peculiar scurrying run that was the speciality of all Partners—an oddly sinuous movement in which the back and head remained more or less parallel to the surface of the ground and the legs appeared to operate almost independently. Though Coney could not have known it, his movements were the evolutionary product of countless generations bred to exploit the peculiarities of the flues. His whiskers gauged to a hairsbreadth the diameter of the capillary vents and he was able to stop, travel backwards, twist and double within confines that would have appeared to challenge the virtuosity of a snake. In the dim mists of their Tarsial past the Partners had been selectively bred as nocturnal hunters, trained to seek out and destroy the rats, but the last rat had been exterminated long ago and no trace of the enemy survived except as the odd archetypal memory that occasionally troubled a Partner's dreams. Nevertheless, the bond which linked them to the Roamers had, if anything, grown stronger with the passage of time. Coney could no more have conceived of a life without Jo, Mel and Bitos than they could. Each was an extension of the other, and in the ecstatic excitement of sharing a successful "tell" lay the only real meaning for a Partner's existence.

Though he was barely conscious of it, Coney was, nonetheless, aware that he was somehow different from the rest of the pack. Outwardly there was only the streak of white on his underbelly to set him apart from the other three in his litter, but inwardly it was a different story. The subconscious censor mechanism which decreed that no Partner should ever attempt to enter the Lost Levels and which in his brother and sisters operated without fail was, in himself, sadly deficient. At the best of times it was little more than an arbitrary reflex, the merest neural twinge which heightened his excitement every time he squeezed his way between the basalt blocks of the abandoned silo and sniffed that extraordinary saltiness on the landward breeze. And there was Mel.

Six months ago when he had first ventured into the Outside, Coney had done something which, did he but know it, no Partner had done for more than two millennia. Nor was that all. Having made his discovery he kept it to himself. In doing this he was, in fact, proving that he was different not in degree but in kind. For a Partner to refrain from making his tell was not only unheard of, it was almost totally meaningless. True, not all tells were successful, but they *were* tells, and they were the Partners' *raison d'être.* Coney's reticence was simply unthinkable. It was as if one of his remote ancestors, having met a rat in the flues, had sniffed noses and set about mutual grooming. Why then had he done it? Partly, no doubt, it was due to the reinforcement his healthy instinct for self-preservation had received as soon as he re-entered the permitted Fringes after that first hesitant sally beyond. He had broken the Law and no good could come of confessing that. For a week he had suffered from loss of appetite and a general debility which, long ago, would no doubt have been diagnosed correctly as the effect of a guilty conscience. Furthermore he was plagued by vivid dreams. Which was where Mel came into it.

Coney's mother had died when her siblings were only ten days old and they would undoubtedly have joined her in the processor had not Jo and Mel taken pity on them and undertaken the arduous task of rearing them by hand. The relationship thus established was extraordinarily close. They were given their names almost before they had acquired separate identities: Coney and Smut the two males; Trig and Flit the females. It soon emerged that all four symbiots were more than ordinarily endowed and, in Coney's case, quite exceptionally. In him the power of telling had been raised to a higher degree than either Jo or her brother had ever experienced. What is more they discovered they had the ability to reciprocate. This was something quite new in Partnership and, like so many discoveries, it was made purely by chance.

One night, shortly after Mel's sixteenth birthday, he and Bitos had come back from a clandestine expedition to a nearby Plant colony. As usual they were wrought up and very full of themselves, though how much of what they recounted to Jo was fact and how much adolescent erotic fantasy was impossible for her to judge. Eventually Mel had crawled into his sleepcell and had, she supposed, fallen asleep. Half an hour later she was shaken awake to hear him informing her that Coney had been reading him. She had assumed, naturally enough, that he was still floating on Plant juice and told him to leave her alone, but his persistence had finally prevailed.

He told her he had been lying awake remembering the raid and the young Plant he had almost plucked at the back of the Temple. If he were telling the truth, the Plant had not been exactly averse to his attentions and had been on the point of submitting when she had realized what he was and had reacted accordingly. Mel had, apparently, been luxuriating retrospectively in the memory when he had become aware that Coney was sharing his pillow. He was on the point of flinging him out when, according to Mel, Coney had told him with excruciating vividness the very incident he had just recounted. So vividly, in fact, that before he had fully realized what was happening, he had spilled. 'And don't tell me it was a dream,' he concluded. 'I'm telling you he *read* me!'

More to shut him up than because she believed him, Jo had called Coney to her, lain back and commanded him to tell her what he had read in Mel. Coney had obediently opened his hold once more. With that extraordinary heightened vividness that was the hallmark of all Coney's tell, Jo found herself living through her brother's adventure in all its dimensions, even to the point of experiencing a vicarious male orgasm herself. It was that which finally convinced her.

Mel watched her twisting and turning under the thin sleep cover. When she was still but for the deep gasping breaths of aftermath he said: 'Well? Do you believe me?'

'Godhole,' she murmured reverently, 'so *that's* what it's like for a man?'

'Except that I didn't have her,' Mel pointed out. 'But you see what Coney's done, don't you?'

Jo still appeared somewhat shaken by her experience. She

stroked Coney's head gingerly. Then she said: 'Let's try if he can read me and tell you. Come on, boy.'

Coney, who seemed to relish being the centre of attention, plonked himself down on her chest and proceeded to lick her nose affectionately. She shifted him up to her pillow, did her best to explain to him what he was to do and then visualized an incident that had occurred when she had stumbled over a little Picking Factor down by the fungus fields. 'Now tell Mel,' she commanded.

Mel scooped up the Partner and they touched heads. A minute later he put him down again and recounted to Jo exactly what had happened to her. 'Well, what do you make of it?' he demanded.

'I don't know,' she confessed. 'We'll have to tell them, won't we?'

'So they can take him away like they did Titus? We won't say a word to anyone. Not yet.'

'Not even to Bitos?'

'Well, let *me* tell him. But he's the only one.'

'All right, Mel. If you say so.'

Thus Coney had been reprieved and, perhaps in some way known only to himself, he read Mel's transgression and recognized in the Clan Leader's son a kindred spirit among the Roamers. Even so he hadn't *told* Mel about the Outside. Not at first. Mel had read that for himself. A Partner's dream? Take it or leave it, brother. Dreams are outside the scope of the Law and we know it, don't we? But this was unlike any Partner dream that Mel had ever read and it seemed to call to him with an imperious, yearning intensity like the whinnying of the glass trumpets at a Plant High Festival. 'Tell me,' he had commanded time and time again. 'Tell, Coney, tell!' And Coney had told, emptying his hold into the boy's mind until Mel too vicariously tasted the salt on the air, sniffed the drowsy fumes of ripening sunwarmed corn and saw the first grains of star-dust pricking through the fathomless evening sky. Was this really just a Partner's dream? Mel wondered and, as he wondered, he too dreamed. And Coney knew that he had Mel's licence to return.

So the secret bond had been struck. While Mel contrived to cover his absence, Coney slipped away into the Lost Levels to return, hours later, with strange fragrant scents adhering to his coat and a hold stuffed full of wonders. Some of these were so incredible that, lacking the experiential evidence to tether them to reality, Mel's credence was stretched to breaking point. Coney's tells of rain, of sun, of clouds, of birds and trees—of the thousand and one natural miracles that Mel's distant ancestors would have taken completely for granted—these were, to Mel himself, little short of terrifying. Had it not been for the ubiquitous machines whose genealogy he recognized in the Handlers and Factors of the Levels, he would probably have written off poor Coney as crazy and handed him over, like Titus, to the Elds for processing. But the Farming Factors and their various menial progeny afforded the vital link between the known and the unknown. As Mel became more and more familiar with that extraordinary region he conceived the insane idea of exploring its marvels for himself. One night, in a stormflash of inspiration, he hit upon the notion of somehow linking such an expedition with his Manhood offering.

At first the sheer audacity of the idea simply overwhelmed him. Columbus planning his voyage to the west was at least aware of the Copernican theorists behind him. Mel had no one. Every Roamer knew that beyond the Lost Levels there was nothing. The Losts *were* the end. No one, so far as he knew, had ever attempted to enter them, let alone returned to tell of it. There were certain things you just didn't talk about—didn't even *speculate* about if you knew what was good for you. All the good Roamer needed to know was there in the Catechism and the Creed. *In the Beginning was God. God built the Levels. God made Man. Man was made by God, for God's purposes. God's Word must be obeyed. God's Ministers must be obeyed. God is the Law.* 'Where *is* God?' Mel had once asked Old Negus and the old man had replied: 'God is everywhere, son.' But Mel knew that wasn't strictly true. There were the Deads, for instance, which God had abandoned and where one day Mel would go with Bitos to make his Manhood offering. There were even parts of the Levels where the God-eyes no longer watched. And there were the vents and flues. For all Mel knew there might be whole areas of the world where God wasn't. Could not Coney's discovery be one of those?

Having conceived his plan he set about laying its groundwork. The utmost caution was necessary for he knew that if any hint of what he intended reached the ears of the Elds they would certainly forbid it, fearful of the Godswrath that might be brought down on their own heads. Nevertheless he had to amass all the information he could if he were to have even a slight hope of succeeding. Accordingly he set to work in a roundabout fashion. First he gleaned the Deads with Seeker and Coney and collected a small trove of the coloured pebbles and metal trinkets which could still be found if the searcher was sufficiently determined. Out of these he fashioned a necklace which he took to the Plant market and traded for a bladder of juice. Then he went to call on Old Negus.

4

The position Old Negus held in the Jewellers' Clan had never been officially defined. There were certain areas, such as the teaching of the Law, which had fallen to him more or less by default, and to him had been assigned the responsibility of preparing boys for their Manhood. But among the other Elds he was regarded as something of a joke. They tolerated him; on occasion they had been known to consult him, and, when things went wrong, they frequently blamed him. His standing was somewhere between unofficial soothsayer and official scapegoat. Nevertheless, everyone admitted that in one sphere at least he held undisputed sway: he was a princely storyteller. No one could tell the Saga of the First Flit like Old Negus and at the annual Greatfoods he would hold the Clans spellbound with his tales of the Kobold and of the ancient wars between the Roamers and the Roberts. But for all that he was a rather disreputable old rag-bag, given to making sour jokes which no one except himself found funny, and frequently he stank abominably. He had always had a soft spot for Mel and had gone out of his way to teach him the Sagas. Mel had been quick to learn and before he was knee-high to a Handler could prattle off the myth cycle far better than most of the Elds, but as he had grown older he had begun to look on the old man with the more critical eyes of adolescence and had of late been a less and less frequent visitor to Negus' van. Now, as he hurried down the Highway in the half-light, he wondered how he could broach the tricky subject of the Lost Levels without arousing the old Eld's suspicions.

For reasons best known to himself, Old Negus always stationed his van some distance away from the Clan's enclave. Not that anyone objected to that but it did serve to underline the ambiguity of his position. You couldn't just drop in casually on him. You either went to see him or you stayed away. Mel reached the ten-branched hydrant, turned off the Highway and picked a path among the heaps of accumulated junk to where a faint glow marked the entrance to the old man's van. An appetizing odour of frying crept down the tunnel towards him. He guessed, rightly, that he wasn't the only visitor Old Negus had had recently. He stepped up to the van and banged it three times with the flat of his hand.

'Wellmet, boy. Come on in. You're just on foodtime. Got some deadmen's fingers here.'

Mel pushed through the bead curtain and ducked into the van. 'Wellmet, Negus. I've brought you some juice.'

'Juice, eh? Well, isn't that something? I was just this minute saying to myself, if I had a mouthful o' juice it would slide these here fingers down a real treat. And here's you step right in with a bladder! Must have read me, eh?'

Mel grinned. 'It didn't take much reading.'

The old man chuckled. 'Sit down, Mel. There's more than enough for two here. How's the family?'

Mel edged himself on to the long seat and put the bladder down on the table before him. 'They're all right,' he said. 'Have you been trading?'

'I've got my friends, boy. They don't all forget Old Negus.' The old man flipped the smoking contents of a pan into a dish and slid it down the table. 'Well, go on, lad,' he prompted. 'Say it.'

'Thank God for this goodfood,' Mel intoned dutifully.

'That's right, Mel. Never forget the grace. God likes to be reminded that we're grateful.'

The Eld rummaged mugs, a couple of forks and a foodstick out of a locker. He broke the stick in two and gave the smaller half to Mel. Then he sat himself down opposite, picked up the bladder, twisted its spout to the pour position and glugged a brimming portion of juice into his own mug and a smaller amount into Mel's. Then, with a wink, he lifted his and drained it to the dregs. Mel sipped and waited for the old man to make a start on the fry.

The Eld belched resonantly, refilled his mug and forked himself a mouthful of the food. 'Go on, boy,' he invited through a crammed mouth. 'Help yourself.'

Mel crunched into one of the crispfried fungus fingers. It was delicious. Neither of them spoke again till the dish was empty. Then the old man belched once more, crooked his little finger and laboriously set about exploring the recesses of his all but toothless gums. 'Now what brings you here, young Mel?' he enquired. 'Pair aching?'

Mel grinned and shook his head.

'Plucked a Plant yet?'

'No,' said Mel.

''Bout ready for one, aren't you?'

Mel shrugged.

The old man scratched his groin and grinned lasciviously. 'Time I was your age, son, I'd had me a dozen. Did I ever tell you about that High Festival in Paris? Seventeen I was. Game for anything. Four of us got ourselves juiced up fit to burst and slipped down the flues into one of their steam baths. What a frazzle that was! Talk about show them what they were missing! 'Course we got flogged raw for it.' He smacked his lips retrospectively. 'Godhole, those were the days, boy!'

'Was the plucking better than—well, among ourselves?' asked Mel.

'I don't know as I'd say that exactly,' said the old man judiciously, helping himself to another mug of juice. 'But it's always the case. The food you're told you can't have is what makes your mouth juice the most.'

'But do the Plants enjoy it, Negus? Jud says they can't.'

''Course he's right, Mel. A Plant's a Plant. But for them it's something new too. They don't do it among themselves like we do.'

'Why can't they, Negus?'

'I didn't say they *can't*, lad. I said they *don't*.' The old man chuckled. 'Godhole, boy, I recall one I had—a fine set-up pluck she was too—for a Plant. Her eyes popped like mushies in a fungus field when she saw the yard I'd come to trade her. Took it too, she did, like a good un. But I was working on her for the best part of half an hour and I still never got her over the top. Just scratching an itch she was. Curious like.' He sighed hugely. 'Still all that's over and done with now for Old Negus. The blood cools off, Mel, and in the end all you're left with is a dusty hold.'

Mel nodded, broke off a bit of foodstick and chewed it thoughtfully. 'Is it true the Plants are dying off, Negus?'

'I've heard talk of it and I daresay there's something in it. A coupla hundred years ago they say there were Plant towns all the way from London to Jerusalem. Even I can recall us Jewellers trading our way through the Levels right down to Rome. We used to van up there for the High Festival then back through Malta and Madrid. And it was fine trading all the way. Ah, those were the days, Mel. You'll never see the Greatways like I've seen 'em. Traders of all kinds up and down. The camps I've seen, boy!'

'But where have they gone to, Negus?'

The old man rootled a thumb in a cavernous, bristling nostril and shrugged. 'Planted, most of 'em, I daresay.'

'Not the Roamers!' Mel was shocked.

'No, not us, boy, though I daresay, if the truth were told, there's more than a few of us who've been tempted. Trade's bad; food's harder to come by; shugging Handlers always chivvying you on; comes a time when you might well ask yourself what's it all for? Where's it get you in the end? Then you might find yourself thinking what it's like being a Plant, and the part of you that's wearied of it all says, Well, why not? And that's one less traveller on the Tracks.'

Mel wondered uneasily if any of the Elds could overhear

their conversation. There were surely limits to what even Old Negus could be allowed to get away with. He nudged the conversation into safer channels. 'But why *are* the Plants dying out, Negus? If you're right there should be more of them, shouldn't there?'

'Godswill, boy.'

"Godswill." How many times had Mel heard *that* when he'd asked a question! It clanged into your face like a vent shield whenever you asked an Eld something he couldn't answer. Well, this time he wasn't going to be put off. 'But, Negus, there must be a *reason*.'

The Eld seemed undecided whether or not to be offended and then finally shrugged. 'Maybe they just don't breed true, Mel. I did hear tell once that they were having trouble with their seed banks.'

'"Seed banks"? What are they, Negus?'

'I'm not rightly sure, but this chap told me that he'd heard how Plant seed was laid down by Godswill at the Beginning. He had hold of some rumour that the Magisters were offering to trade pardons for a prisoner's spill. I never heard no more about it. Don't know as I'd have cared for that sort of trading anyway. Now, when I might be open to a proposition, I haven't got any seed left to trade.'

'Plants aren't *born* planted, are they?'

'I never saw one born, boy. Did you?'

'Of course not.'

'Then how do you know they are?'

'Are what?'

'Born.'

Mel gaped. Was he being serious?

'What's the youngest Plant you've ever seen, Mel? Ten years? Twelve?'

'About ten, I suppose. But I've never been inside a hive.'

'Never seen one titting her sucker?'

'No.'

'Nor a bigbelly?'

Mel shook his head.

'Ever wondered why?'

Mel shrugged. 'I just haven't thought about it before. I suppose they have them in the hives and keep them there till they're big enough to go out by themselves.' A thought struck him. 'Well, we trade toys to them, don't we?'

'We do, Mel.'

'Well, then . . .'

'I didn't say they didn't *have* suckers. I was just putting it to you that maybe they weren't born like we are?'

Mel laughed incredulously. 'What other way is there?'

The old man hitched a ragged eyebrow. 'Spawn beds,' he offered.

'You're not serious.'

'Or something on the same lines.'

The concept was so outrageous that Mel burst out laughing.

Negus grinned and helped himself to more juice. 'And now how about telling me why you're here,' he suggested affably.

Mel's mirth died on his lips.

The old man squinnied at him speculatively over the rim of his mug. 'Manhood bothering you?'

Mel shook his head.

'There's something though,' said the Eld. 'Ask away.'

'How old are you, Negus?'

'Eighty-five—give or take a couple either way.'

'You've vanned the Levels all your life, haven't you?'

'That's right.'

'Have you ever gleaned for trove in the High Fringes?'

'Aye, lad. Once or twice.'

Mel swallowed and felt his heart stumble. 'Negus, what do you know about the Lost Levels?'

Negus choked explosively over his juice, clenched his fist and thumped it against his forehead to ward off the evil eye. Mel watched him apprehensively.

'Godhole, boy, you'll be the death of me yet!'

Mel poured the old man a fresh mugful of juice, waited till the stringy old throat had stopped rippling, then said: 'But I suppose people *have* gone into them, haven't they?'

'Madmen,' muttered Negus.

'What happened to them?'

'Poof! Burnt to ashes.'

'How do you know?'

The old man lapped his tongue across his wet lip. 'Because I saw it happen, that's how.'

Mel's eyes widened perceptibly. 'You *saw* it! Godstruth?'

Negus nodded gloomily.

'What happened?'

'Just like I said. One second there—the next, white ash. I couldn't see clear for months after.'

'Where did this happen, Negus?'

'Way off along the Greatways. Near Leeon.'

'Long ago?'

'Must be more'n fifty years now. But a man doesn't forget a thing like that in a hurry. Poor old Barney.'

'Barney! Wasn't he the one you . . . ?'

'Aye, that's him. My first blood mate. Close on ten years we vanned together. He was with me that time in Paris. Charm the sensors out a Factor could Barney. 'Sfact, boy, I seen him do it.' The old man's eyes filled with rheumy tears. 'Godstruth, Mel, that man was a magician. He had this little old whistle he'd made and he'd go off down the beds of an evening and call the Factors to him. Just by whistling. For ten years we never went hungry. They used to bring us whole trays of stuff. "Love offerings" old Barney called them. Yet I never heard a thing. The Partners could though. I'd see 'em pricking up their ears and I'd know old Barney was down at the beds again. Sure enough, half an hour later he'd march in and dump a sack down on the van floor. I tell you, Mel, we lived like kings in those days! Kings!'

'How did he come to . . . ?'

Negus shrugged. 'He got some crazy notion in his head. 'S funny thing, Mel, you and Mark sometimes remind me of Barney. Same dreamy look—as though you're both half way to Jerusalem. Hey, d'you remember when I was teaching you the Sagas, eh?'

Mel let him ramble on for a while then brought him back to the subject. 'What notion *did* Barney get into his head, Negus?'

'How should I know, boy? It was just a load of crazy talk.'

Mel took a chance. 'About the Outside?'

The old man's eyes suddenly narrowed into shrewd slits. 'Come again?'

'When Barney talked crazy was it about the Outside?'

'What's that?'

Mel pointed up to the van roof. 'Somewhere up there. Beyond The Losts.'

'How'd you come by such crazy talk, boy? Have you been at a Plant High or something? That's where they spawn that sort of blasphemy.'

Mel was not going to be diverted now. 'Was Barney trying to get there when he was killed, Negus?'

'Get where?' grizzled the old man. 'I don't know what you're talking about.'

'Through the Lost Levels to the Outside.'

'Godhole, boy. How should I know?'

'You were with him, weren't you?'

Negus' eyes leaked again. 'Aye,' he muttered. 'I was with him.'

'Well, didn't he tell you what he was doing?—Where he was trying to get to?'

The old man was silent.

'He must have said *something*,' persisted Mel.

Negus sighed. When at last he spoke he seemed hardly aware that Mel was listening. 'Barney found a way of managing the Handlers. Don't ask me how he did it. It was some sort of music thing he'd made and there were all sorts of bits of looking-glass and stuff in it. But it worked. He couldn't make them come to him like he could some of the Factors, but he could stop them. The first time he tried it out we was down in Spain. We hijacked a juicer. Trouble was we'd never planned what to do with the stuff. Still, it kept us going nicely for a coupla months. If we'd acted sensible we'd have been set for life, but that was never Barney's way. Life for him was just one long Highway of Challenges. Pick something: do it; then pick something harder still and do that. In the end there was only one thing left.'

'The Lost Levels,' murmured Mel.

'Aye, the Losts. The biggest shugging Challenge of them all.'

'What *did* happen, Negus?'

'We had a fight and he went off on his own. I guessed where he was headed and I went after him. I caught up with him in the High Fringes. He wouldn't listen to me, Mel. He just didn't seem to care what happened to him. He'd stripped right down to his naked skin and he went right on up to the barrier and just climbed over. Talk about High Festival! Lights started going off like flaming crackers. I near shugged myself I was so scared. But old Barney he just looked back at me and grinned. Then a Godhole begins to bawl—"Go back! This Level is forbidden! Go back!" And I tell you, Mel, old Barney looked right up at it and shouted: "*I am a man!*" Godstruth, boy, it was the Sagas all over again, only Barney didn't have Ulf's golden armour! Then the old Godhole comes again: "This Level is not for man! Go back!" Barney was walking up a sort of ramp by then and he lifted up his arms like this'—Negus stretched his arms out over the table and turned his hands palm uppermost—'and he sang out: "*Everything is for man!*" For as long as it takes to count up to ten there wasn't a sound and then the Godhole just said sort of quietly: "Yes. *Even death.*" Godstruth I can hear it now! "*Even death.*" That's when it happened. A light so bright I was struck blind and a roar like a hundred freighters down the Tracks. That was the last I ever saw of Barney—the last *anyone* ever saw of him.'

Mel let out his held breath. 'You *saw* him killed?'

'That's what I'm telling you, isn't it? No man ever died braver.'

'But if you were blinded . . . ?'

'I was blinded all right. If a Trash Factor hadn't found me I'd have wandered around the Fringes till I starved. I didn't see properly again for a year and I had headaches and shakes for longer 'n that. 'S though I'd been cursed. Hair fell out; couldn't keep food down: couldn't pluck; couldn't anything. So now you know what's in store for you, lad, if you try poking around up there.'

Mel frowned. 'Why didn't Barney try to get round instead of going straight in?'

''Cos he was crazy,' Negus grunted. 'He had this notion that the Losts was all superstition—that you only needed to show the Godhead you had a right to be there and that you weren't scared and nothing would happen to you. Well, he learnt the hard way.'

'I wish I'd known him,' said Mel.

'Aye, you'd have made a good pair,' muttered Negus. 'Two funerals for the price of one. No, lad, the Lost Levels aren't for the likes of us.'

From the Highway came the groan of the curfew warning. Mel stood up and swigged off the remains of his juice. 'Thanks for the food, Negus. And for the talk too.'

'Any time, Mel. You know where to find me.'

With his hand on the curtain Mel paused and looked down at the old Eld. 'Barney *did* believe in the Outside, didn't he, Negus?'

Old Negus cocked his head on one side and tapped a forefinger against the side of his nose. 'No, you've got it wrong, lad,' he wheezed. 'It wasn't the "Outside" Barney was after, it was somewhere he called "Haven". Now do us both a favour and forget it.'

5

That night Mel lay awake for a long time turning over in his mind all he had gleaned from the old man. When it was finally sifted out he found himself left holding one enigmatic fragment that didn't seem to make sense whichever way he considered it. When he had broached the subject of the Lost Levels Negus had first accused him of talking crazy, which was understandable, and had then charged him with picking up blasphemies from a Plant High, which was not. Or was it just another way of saying "crazy talk"? Mel's knowledge of the Plants and their peculiar ritual was limited largely to hearsay—the Clan gossip that all the youngsters picked up and embellished in order to enhance their prestige among themselves—but what did they really *know*? For the first time in his life he found himself wondering exactly why it was that the Roamers affected to despise the Plants. Was it simply because they depended on the Plants for their meagre livelihood? Certainly if there were no Plants to trade with it was difficult to see how the Roamers could survive. But he guessed that the real reason lay deeper than that and that it was somehow bound up with the way in which Jud and the other Elds spat surreptitiously after they had chaffered with a male Plant. He recalled the way in which his father had once rounded on him and growled: 'They're not men, Mel. Having a yard and a pair don't make you a man. It's up here, lad.' And he'd spread his thumb and middle finger and pressed them up against the temples of Mel's young forehead on the spot where the Plants had their silver buds. 'That's where you're a man, son, and don't you forget it.'

Mel never had forgotten it. Many of the other things Jud had told him he had since privately questioned and discarded, but that had stuck fast. Now he was prepared to weigh even that. In the darkness of the sleepcell he lifted a hand and with his fingertips traced the bony ridges of his brow and the soft declivity of his temple. He thought uneasily of Barney striding to his death with the cry: '*I am a man!*' What did it mean? What *was* a man? One by one he called up the eight male Elds of the Clan and reviewed them in his mind's eye. What had they in common? Black-bearded Jud, his father; strong as a Handler; surly; given to dark, bitter moods during which you spoke to him at your peril and risked a sudden unmerited clout that sent you sprawling: Redeye with his quick, loose grin and broken teeth; virtuoso warbler; master mechanic of the vans; Brod Seedspiller, Bitos' father; mighty of yard and pair; with a laugh like the curfew siren and a subtle knack with jewellery that had made his name a byword in the markets and insured that, while his anvil was ringing, the Clan would always feed: the brothers Lefty and Rill; not much given to talking; master colourists both but miserly with the secrets of their craft; sometimes lying mushed for days together in their van. Karl the clown, light-fingered, quick-talking prince of traders who lived to chaffer and—so the story went—had once wept because a Plant had paid him what he asked first time: disreputable old Negus: and finally Mark—'Dark Mark', jack of all trades and something more; a strange blend of Jud's moodiness, Redeye's music and Karl's flickering wit; a breaker of hearts who knew how to whisper any women into parting her knees yet tied to none; a wanderer in the Deep Levels, a dreamer and a poet whose brown eyes seemed always to be smiling at some secret joke. Assuredly all these were men, yet what had they in common that they did not share with the Plants? Was it only the absence of the silver buds, or was there something else, something that made you a Roamer, something that dwelt in your blood and drove you out restlessly down the Highways seeking for you knew not what? He was still no nearer to an answer when at last he drifted off into an uneasy sleep.

His dreams were troubled by taunting visions of the young Plant he'd fondled in the alleyway behind the Temple, and he woke aching and resentful. It was still half-light when Jo called to him that Jud wanted to see him. Mel delayed as long as he dared then, grumbling bitterly, kicked off his cover, dragged on his clothes and stumbled down the steps and across the enclave to his father's van. Inside he found Mark and Jud pulling tight the straps on a back-pack. Mirl, Jud's cellmate, handed her stepson a steaming mug of brew and smiled at him. Mel took it, nodded his thanks, and waited for his father to speak first.

Jud tugged the last buckle tight, grunted, and gave Mel a brief nod. 'You took your time.'

Mel shrugged. 'I'm here.'

'You're going to Bristol with Mark.'

'What for?'

'You're taking this lot to the market. Mark'll tell you the rest on the way. You can jump a freighter on twenty-two.'

Mel's eyes widened. Something was on. But what? Had they been ordered to flit? Mark shouldered the pack and muttered something in a low voice to Jud. Outside the light was up to three-quarters. Mel gulped at his brew and felt it scald down his gullet. Mirl handed him a small foodsack, wished him Godspeed, and then they were outside hurrying towards the Highway, while behind them the firstsmoke of the vans wisped up into the high vents overhead.

Mark moved with the easy, loping stride of the born Leveller, his head slightly bent and his brown eyes darting from side to side, alert alike to danger and gleanings. In fifteen minutes they had descended five Levels and, apart from the ubiquitous Maintenance Factors, had seen nothing. Mel was aware of a gnawing pain under his ribs but gritted his teeth and did his best to ignore it.

As they stepped off the last Inter-Level ramp Mark turned to him with a grin. 'These things were once called "Flow-Ways". Did you know that, Mel?'

Mel shook his head. 'What's it mean?'

'What it says, I suppose. You just stood on them and they flowed you down.'

Mel suspected he was having his leg pulled but Mark pointed to a hair-fine crack that ran down the edge of the ramp and joined another at right angles at the Highway Level. 'I reckon that's where it ended. And see this?' He indicated the metal pipe that had served them as a handguide. 'Notice anything?'

Mel peered at it. It looked exactly like a thousand others he'd seen up and down the Levels. 'No,' he admitted.

'Well, here it's worn quite smooth, but there'—Mark pointed to where the pipe bent from the horizontal to the vertical—'it's still rough.'

Mel shrugged. 'What about it?'

'How long do you reckon it'd take you to smooth down a bit of rough mantine using just your bare hand?'

Mel frowned. 'You mean . . .?'

'There's a lot of things we don't know, Mel.'

Mel looked up at the ramp wandering above them, then round at the colossal arch of the Highway and suddenly, unaccountably, he shivered. 'But what's happened to them, Mark? Where have they all gone? Was it the Deads?'

Mark hefted up the straps of his pack and shrugged. 'Who knows?'

'Were they Plants?'

'Most of 'em, I daresay.'

Mel nodded. 'Negus says there were once Plant towns all along the Greatways. He says the Roamers used to trade right down to Jerusalem.'

'I've heard his stories.'

'Is it true, do you think?'

Mark pursed his lips noncommittally. 'Times change, Mel. A lot of the smaller towns have moved into the Citadels. There's quite a few Levels been closed down, you know.'

'The Deads, you mean?'

'They must've been that way since near the Beginning. No, I mean in the Deeps. The Redding workbeds have been closed off since last Flit.'

'Who says so?'

'Fargal—the man we're going to see. He's got a load of chippings he wants to trade off. A Factor brought in the samples last night. Where were you?'

'Down with Old Negus.'

Mark grunted. 'Old Feedguts, you mean. Come on, lad, we don't want to miss our jump.'

Mel had ridden the freighters since he was eight years old. It was one of those quasi-illegal Clan practices that distinguished the Roamers from the rest of the Levellers. From time to time there would be a Security drive aimed at stamping it out; one or two unfortunates would be dragged before the Magisters and given an exemplary flogging, but, apart from making the rest more wary, such measures had little effect. For some months now the heat had been off and there was little attendant risk apart from the ever-present threat to life and limb. So long as you picked your spot with care and acted decisively when the moment came the ride was yours for the taking.

Mark, who had recently reconnoitred the area, led the way down the steeply spiralled inspection flange of a main vent and then ducked off along a gantry that spanned the freight tracks. Peering down Mel saw a sub-line snaking off at a tangent and guessed why this point had been chosen,

They did not have long to wait. A tell-tale pricking in their ear drums was followed, almost immediately, by a distant reverberating rumble. Mark tested the security of the back straps and nodded to Mel. They wriggled over the gantry rail and crouched side by side in the shadow. The noise grew louder. A thrust of warm air pushed like a cushion into their backs and then there was a long, sustained hissing. Mel, squinting under his arm-pit, saw the freighter emerge from the tunnel and glide below them, slowing perceptibly for the junction. One section flowed beneath them; a second; a third —'Now!' yelled Mark.

For a sickening moment Mel's clawing fingers slid wild over the smooth surface, then they had closed on the seam ridge of the flexible coupling canopy. With a grateful sigh, he eased himself down into the cosy hammock beside Mark and listened to the scream of the floaters picking up. Mark winked at him, slid his arm free of the pack and circled his shoulder-blades to restore circulation. Then he put his mouth close to Mel's ear and yelled: 'Sucker's play, eh?'

Mel nodded. 'How long will it take?'

Mark pointed to his ear.

'How long?' screamed Mel.

Mark held up one finger to signify an hour and then they both lay back, pillowed their heads on their hands and gazed up at the flickering roof of the tunnel. Riding the freighter was notorious for restricting conversation.

Fifty minutes later they glided into the Bristol freighter terminal. It was the first time Mel had been there but he had seen other terminals and if this one differed from those it was only in details too insignificant to be apparent. The place was literally crawling with Factors of every conceivable size and shape. There was even one hovering in the air overhead. Mel pointed it out to Mark who nodded. 'It won't bother with us. It's the patrols we've got to watch out for. You keep close to me.'

They slid down into the siding and hurried over the oil-blotched trackway to the loading bays. In spite of Mark's assurance Mel kept a wary eye on the little airborne Factor which was whisking back and forth overhead like a frenzied dragonfly. 'What keeps it up, Mark?'

'Floaters, I s'pose. Look out!' He grabbed Mel's arm and dragged him precipitately into an empty freight car. 'Pluck our luck,' he muttered. 'Did they see us?'

Mel peered cautiously out. 'No, I don't think so.'

'What are they doing?'

'Just standing there. Now they're talking to a Sweeper.'

'Can you see any Plants?'

Mel peeked again. 'No.' A minute passed. 'The Handlers are going off now,' he reported. 'I think it's safe.'

'All right, we'll chance it. Now just walk naturally, as though we've got a perfect right to be here. Up the ramp and past the bays. If one of them calls out to you, pretend you haven't heard it. But if you *do* get stopped, act dumb. Understand?'

Mel nodded.

'Right. On your way, lad.'

They emerged once more and this time traversed the depot without incident. At the top of the ramp Mark waved down a Haulage Factor and they rode it up the Intermediate Levels to the Great Westway.

The man they had come to meet had not yet arrived so Mark left word with a Lottery Hawker in the market and took Mel into a foodbar to wait for him. There were one or two Plants sitting at the tables and they eyed the Roamers with that peculiar abstracted stare that Mel always associated with them. A little Server bustled up, recited the bill of fare in a piping treble and took their order. While they were waiting for it to arrive Mark unfastened his pack and, with a wink at Mel, set a finger-high metal tripod on the table before him. On top of the tripod he pivoted a mirror-ball the size of a hen's egg which he set spinning with a flick of his finger. Mel grinned. The light pricked off the facets of the ball in a tiny irregular coruscation, wholly entrancing to the eye. Glancing covertly round Mel saw one of the Plants nudging her neighbour. Balanced on its needlepoint the little ball spun on, seemingly tireless, *wink-wink-wink* flicker *wink-wink*. The Plant murmured something to her companion, stood up and moved quietly across to the corner where Mark and Mel were sitting. 'Excuse me,' she said. 'What is that?'

Mark slowly raised his head and regarded her sombrely. 'This, ma'am, is the Shrine of Arfaxis.'

'Oh.' Her grey eyes blinked slowly. 'What does it do?'

'Do? It simply *is*, ma'am.'

'It is . . .' she hesitated '. . . very beautiful.'

Mark shrugged. 'It points the Way, ma'am.'

'"The Way"? What is that?'

'The Way to Knowledge of the Self. Those who feel themselves drawn to it are tangled in the Web of Fate.'

'I do not understand.'

The little ball was slowing now, beginning to wobble on its pivot. Mark stopped it with one finger and dexterously set it spinning again. 'Arfaxis is the Arbiter of Fate, ma'am. But perhaps you are among those fortunate few to whom the Future is of no interest. . . .'

The grey eyes blinked again. 'You are a fortune-teller?'

'I am a Roamer.'

She lifted her gaze from the twinkling ball with an almost visible effort. 'A Roamer,' she murmured. 'They say you have strange powers.'

Mark inclined his head in a bow of mock deprecation.

'Such as they are, my poor gifts are yours to command. Would you and your friend care to join us?'

The Plant, whom Mel guessed to be in her middle years, nodded and beckoned her companion. At a sign from Mark Mel fetched two more stools. The women sat down and regarded the Roamer gravely.

Mark removed the little sphere and its tripod from the table centre, slipped them into his pack and brought out a small leather bag which was threaded at its throat with a coloured thong. He handed this bag to the Plant, told her to take it in her left hand, to shake it, to invert it and then to release the cord.

In a small cascade, twelve little glittering tetrahedrons tumbled on to the table centre. Mark's long fingers danced swiftly among them, flicking them into their separate colour groups of red and blue. This done he smiled and waited. Under the table Mel felt the Eld's foot tap his ankle. Leaning to the woman he whispered: 'You must give him two tokens.'

The transaction completed, Mark slipped into his routine. Turning up the little pyramids one by one to expose the rune engraved on each base, he wove his elaborate tissue from the warp and woof of Past and Future. Whenever, by some slight movement of her eyes or lips, the Plant betrayed that he had hit upon a truth, he probed skilfully until he had exposed it. Mel had assisted him many times but was invariably fascinated anew by the Eld's skill even though he knew each reading was five parts shrewd character analysis, four parts undiluted nonsense, and one part sheer chance. He knew too that Mark always based his patter on the initial turn up of the runes. At least to that extent the Seer believed in what he saw.

Mark concluded the readings and graciously bade his clients farewell. After they had gone he gave Mel one of the four tokens and beckoned to the Server. When the little machine trundled up Mark slotted home a second token, whereupon the robot slid back its hot hatch and allowed them to help themselves to their syrup cakes and choy.

While they were eating, two Roamers, a man and a woman, entered the foodbar, caught sight of Mark and came across. They exchanged wellmet with the Eld, nodded to Mel and sat down on the stools the Plants had vacated. Mark introduced Mel, ordered choy for the newcomers and asked them where they were vanned.

'In the Precinct,' said the man who called himself Fargal. 'We've got to be away by curfew. You got the samples?'

Mark delved into his pack and produced a small, grubby bundle which he handed over. 'How much more is there?'

'Half a bushel. That's a fair sample.'

'And your price?'

Fargal flicked a hand open and shut four times.

Mark whistled faintly between his teeth.

'It's the last there'll be,' said Fargal. 'They've closed off the whole Level, ain't they, Dol?'

The woman nodded.

'Look,' said the man, and taking the woman's right wrist he turned her hand palm upwards on the table. The seared, flash-burnt flesh lay pouched and wrinkled in grey-white folds across the fingertips and down the heel of the palm. The woman regarded it dumbly as though it were no part of her. Mel winced.

'We've got to pay for cure,' said Fargal. 'What use is that hand as it is?'

'What happened?'

'Like I said, they closed it off. We'd left a pick at the workings and Dol went back for it. When she weren't home at curfew I went to look for her. Found her lying at the top of the ramp.'

'Didn't they warn you?'

Fargal sneered. 'What's a Roamer more or less to them shuggers? Trash, that's all we are. Trash.'

Mark gnawed his lower lip. 'I don't know, Fargal. Twenty's a heavy load. Jud was reckoning on a top fifteen.'

'Burn cure's fifteen, Mark. And we're no floaters. We've got to eat too.'

The Server came up with their drinks and Mark handed them round. Mel knew that Mark would pay what Fargal was asking. The only one of the Clan who might have been able to ignore that ravaged hand was Karl, and Jud in his wisdom hadn't sent him. He smiled shyly at the woman. 'Are you Loners?' he asked.

'Aye,' she nodded. 'And how old are you, boy?'

'Sixteen.'

'Yard high?'

'Next month.'

She smiled at him, laid her good left hand along his thigh and pinched him gently. 'Well up, lad.'

Mel grinned his thanks and, absurdly, felt himself blushing.

Fargal laughed, wiped his red lips with the back of his hand and said: 'I've got a lonely bladder waiting for us back in the van. Let's go.'

6

Part of the Temple Precinct had been ordained Roamer sanctuary for longer than anyone could remember, but the duration of a stay was always strictly limited and the Handlers were there to see the rules were obeyed. The Fargals were pass-checked at the gateway, warned that they were to be clear by curfew and then allowed in. Mark and Mel were scanned, asked their business, and handed temporary bracelet passes by a Clerking Factor. That done they were as free to come and go as any Roamer ever was in a Plant Citadel.

They followed Fargal across the paved area to the residence yards. Four other vans were docked in the bays. Half a dozen youngsters were engaged in a ritual game whose ancestry stretched back along the Greatways to when the world was young. Two mangy-looking Partners were tethered by lengths of twine to a metal pillar next to Fargal's van and, as Mel mounted the steps, one lifted a hind leg and scratched its ear furiously.

Fargal ushered them into the van and dragged a basket out of a sleepcell. It was half full of the coloured mosaic chippings that the Clan used as the basis for much of their jewellery. Mark plunged his hand in, withdrew it and rolled the stones in his palm. 'Nice, eh?' said Fargal.

Mark grunted, tipped his handful back and plunged his arm in again.

'They're not salted,' grinned Fargal and picked one up. 'There's a beauty for you, eh? Worth any Plant's token.'

'What was the seam like?' asked Mark.

'Pure virgin. We'd been pecking around for a week before we struck it. A Factor put us on to it. If we'd found it a week earlier I reckon we'd have been set up for six months. We took that lot in a single session.'

'All right,' said Mark. 'You've made your sale.'

The two men clasped hands and while Mark counted out the tokens, Fargal told Dol to fetch the juice. At that moment the doorway darkened and a girl entered carrying an armful of foodsticks and a jug. She darted a quick look at the two visitors, gave a tiny bob of her silvery head and moved past them down to the far end of the van. 'How about a wellmet then, Frankie?' demanded Fargal.

The girl muttered something and Mel heard Dol address some remark to Fargal out of the side of her mouth. Mark said: 'If it's all the same to you I'll leave this stuff with you for a couple of hours. We've got some tradings to unload while we're here.'

'It'll be safe enough,' said Fargal. 'But don't forget we're due out by curfew. What are you selling?'

'Rings and necklaces mostly. A couple of chaplets.'

'Mind if I look?'

'Help yourself,' said Mark. He lifted the market roll out of his pack, untied it, and with a flick of his wrist released it across the table. The jewellery squirmed and glittered as it came to rest, filling the van with a wealth of little fragile rainbows. Mark lifted a chaplet and let it dangle from his fingers. 'Hurry-hurry-hurry,' he chanted in the familiar pedlar's sing-song. 'Here are frozen dreams to buy. Teardrop or hearts-ease! Magic's in the web of it! Hurry-hurry-hurry!'

Fargal chuckled. 'Very nice,' he said admiringly. 'That's Seedspiller's handiwork or I'm a Factor.'

Mel noticed that the girl had moved forward and was gazing with parted lips at the chaplet which was still swinging gently from Mark's fingers. On an impulse he reached out, lifted the filigree and beckoned to her. She came to him like a sleepwalker. Grinning, he arranged the band round her forehead, while her eyes, as blue as aquamarines, gazed deep into his. He pushed back the blonde hair from her broad brow and, as he did so, his mouth opened in dumb astonishment.

'It suits her,' said Mark. 'Come on down to the market with us, lass. We'll use you as a model.'

She shook her head, but Dol said: 'Yes, go on, Frankie. I'll manage here all right.'

The girl turned beseeching eyes on Fargal.

'Sure. Why not?' he said. 'Drink up, lads, or you'll miss the best of your buyers.'

They found themselves a vacant pitch at one end of the colonnade and while Mark spread out the roll and settled down cross-legged with Frankie beside him, Mel set about adorning the girl with necklaces and rings. Before he had finished, a small crowd had collected. These attracted others and soon the three Roamers were the centre of a jostling craning circle.

Frankie knelt as still as a statue, bare to the waist, gazing out unseeing at some point in the remote distance. The slight rise and fall of her breast made the light ripple and quiver among the polished facets of the necklaces. She looked like a small, barbaric princess officiating at some ancient and arcane rite, while the Plants competed among themselves for the privilege of stripping her bare.

Within half an hour Mark had sold everything down to the last ring at prices which would surely have evoked admiration even from Karl. While Frankie donned her smock Mel bundled up the empty roll. Mark counted out five tokens and handed them to Frankie. 'You brought us good fortune, lass. We should have you with us every time. Ever done it before?'

Frankie shook her head.

'She's a natural,' said Mel. 'The stuff looked as if it had been made for her, didn't it?'

Mark nodded. 'Who gave you that skin, Frankie? Not Fargal, I'll be bound.'

The girl corded her smock in at her waist and said nothing.

'We could certainly use it,' said Mark. 'Or doesn't independence appeal to you?'

'I'm not Fargal's,' she said.

'Whose are you then? Dol's?'

'I just van with them.'

Mark strapped up the pack and hoisted it on to his shoulder. 'You could take a place with us if you're interested.'

'I'll think about it.'

Mark laughed and turned to Mel. 'I've got a bit of private business to attend to. I'll see you back at Fargal's in two hours.'

Mel nodded and watched the Eld shoulder his way into the

4

throng and vanish in the direction of the taverns. 'Are you going home now, Frankie?' he asked.

The girl tested her tokens deliberately, one by one, between her white teeth. 'Maybe,' she said guardedly.

'We could go and look at the Galleries for a bit,' he suggested.

'Go on then.'

'You come too.'

'Who wants to see a lot of stupid Plants getting high?'

Mel shrugged. 'All right. You say somewhere.'

Frankie hazed into the middle distance. 'There's the Random Arcades,' she murmured.

'You must be crazy!' he protested. 'You know they throw out Roamers as soon as they spot us!'

Frankie smiled faintly and clinked her tokens. 'Can you read the wheels?' she asked.

'I don't know,' Mel admitted. 'I've never tried.'

'I think I can.' She turned the blue blaze of her astonishing eyes full upon him. 'Shall we try, Mel?'

'All right,' he agreed uneasily. 'If you want to. How do we get there?'

She seized him by the hand and set off at a quick trot down the colonnade, her bare feet whispering over the translucent tesserae and the long silvergold braid of her hair bouncing across her shoulders. They turned off down a narrow alleyway, crossed a small square in which a light-fountain tirelessly shook out its gossamer rainbows, and then ducked into a subway. Here Frankie paused for breath, released Mel's hand and pointed to an arched entrance over which two floating dice cubes slowly revolved. From the dimly lit interior drifted the sound of plangent music. They waited until a group of gamblers appeared and then followed them in.

It took a moment or two for Mel's eyes to grow accustomed to the subdued illumination. When they did he found himself in a long, low-ceilinged hall around the walls of which, like exotic fish in a series of aquarium tanks, swam mysterious coloured lights and symbols. In front of each window stood a line of Plants gazing with rapt attention at the swirling configurations within. There was a constant metallic tinkle of tokens tumbling into chutes, and now and again a muted exhalation greeted a larger win.

Frankie twitched at Mel's sleeve and drew him across to one of the windows where two Plants had just vacated their place. Mel gazed into the flickering depths before him and tried to fathom some significant pattern behind the shifting web of light. As far as he could see there was none. As he watched the lights faded one by one leaving a solitary symbol which seemed to hang, momentarily suspended, like a single water-drop, before it too dimmed and vanished. A few tokens trickled into a chute at the far end of the line and then the lights were swirling off into a new vortex.

In the gloom beside him Frankie pushed one of her tokens into a slot, selected a button from the array before her and pushed it. Mel fingered the token Mark had given him in the foodbar, hesitated, and decided against it. The lights dimmed and faded as before, except that this time a new symbol was isolated. A moment later Frankie's chute was dancing with the tokens she had won.

Glancing sideways at her Mel noticed that she was leaning forward so that her forehead rested against the transparent window. Her eyes were closed. Even as he watched she frowned, moved back, and taking up the tokens she had won fed them all, one after another, into a single slot. Without further ado he thrust his own token into the corresponding slot on his own panel and pressed the button she had selected.

She won again and as Mel scooped up his winnings he was aware of voices whispering in the gloom around him and caught the word "Roamer". He pulled at Frankie's arm but she either would not or could not heed him. Her forehead was back against the window. 'Frankie,' he pleaded. 'Let's go now.'

But she was far away from him in some strange psychokinetic world of her own and it is doubtful whether she could have heard him even if she had wished. A moment later he found himself shouldered roughly to one side and a Plant with hungry eyes was avidly watching Frankie's choice. As soon as she had made her selection he crammed a fistful of tokens into the identical slot on the panel Mel had been occupying.

Again Mel reached for her arm but the Plant knocked his hand aside and growled: 'Let her ride it, fool.'

Frankie won twice more and then a light above the window started to flash.

The Plant scooped up his winnings, grunted: 'Flit!' and melted away into the gloom.

Mel seized hold of Frankie and dragged her back from the window by main force. She reeled against him drunkenly and spilled tokens rolled around their feet. 'Come on,' he panted. 'Quick! They're on to us!'

The whole window was now flashing on and off, splashing light across the Arcade and a metal voice intoned: 'Interference with Number 16! Attendants, please! Interference with Number 16! Patrons please remain in their places!'

Searching desperately for a way of escape, Mel glimpsed a curtained doorway and hustled Frankie through it. An unidentifiable Factor trundled towards them, bleeping indignantly, but Mel dodged round it, dragged Frankie after him along the passageway and up a spiral ramp. They staggered out into a back alley just as the metal grille clattered down to seal off the doorway behind them. 'Godhole,' he gasped, 'are you *trying* to get us flayed? Where do we go?'

She looked round her bemusedly, shook her head as if to clear it, and then pointed down the lane. They ran until their legs would carry them no farther then ducked into a shadowed archway where they subsided panting and listened for sounds of pursuit. When she was sure they were safe Frankie thrust her hand into the slit pocket of her smock and pulled out a brimming handful of tokens. 'Here,' she sighed. 'Take them.'

Mel shook his head. 'They're yours. You won them.'

'Keep them for me,' she said, thrusting them at him. 'If Fargal finds out what I've been up to he'll skin me.'

'Then you *have* done it before?'

'Not like that, Mel. I could have made it do anything—*anything*!'

Mel raised his hand and pushed back the tumbled hair from her forehead. 'What *are* you, Frankie?'

She twisted her head away and would not meet his eyes. 'A Roamer,' she muttered.

'What Clan?'

'Loner.'

He shook his head. 'Fargal's a Loner, but you said you weren't his.'

'He's not the only one.'

'How long have you vanned with him?'

'Who do you think you are?' she muttered. 'A Magister or something?'

'I just wondered.'

She glanced up at him from beneath her lowered lashes then slowly raised her left hand and rested her fingertips on her temple. 'It's these, isn't it?' she said. 'You saw them in the van.'

In the dim light that penetrated the archway the tiny star-shaped cicatrice stood out faintly paler upon the pale flesh. Mel swallowed and then nodded. 'I'm sorry,' he said. 'It's really none of my business.'

With a tiny abstracted gesture her fingertip traced the outline of the scar while her eyes brimmed with slow tears. Mel put out his hand and laid it gently on her arm. 'I'm sorry, Frankie,' he repeated.

But she was as far beyond the reach of his contrition now as she had previously been beyond his call in the Arcade. She seemed to be the sole inhabitant of a little private hell of her own loneliness. Even the tears which swam in her eyes did not flow down her cheeks but stayed to transform her eyes into vast, luminous pools of unhappiness.

'Can't you talk about it?'

'What's the use? Talking won't make me belong, will it?'

To Mel these were uncharted seas; he trusted to dead-reckoning and plunged on. 'But you *aren't* a Plant, are you, Frankie? Not now, I mean. Now you're one of us.'

'Am I?'

Was she? Mel groped among unfamiliar concepts. Was a Roamer just someone who felt themselves to be one? Even someone who had once been planted? He guessed what Jud's opinion would be and how it would be expressed, but he wasn't Jud and, anyhow, hadn't Mark offered her vanroom? 'Of course, you're a Roamer,' he affirmed and added, with a flash of inspiration, 'that's why they unplanted you, isn't it?'

The corners of Frankie's lips trembled into a faint smile. 'What do you really *know* about the Plants, Mel?'

Mel shrugged. 'Not much,' he admitted uneasily. 'They don't have their suckers like we do, do they?'

'Is that all?'

'They don't pluck.'

She shook her head and chuckled in spite of herself.

Mel coloured. 'Well, go on then, tell me,' he challenged.

Frankie brushed her eyes with the back of her hand. 'Look,' she said, 'what's the one thing every Roamer notices about the Plants?'

'Well, the buds, of course.'

'Yes, the buds. Do you know what they're for? What they *do*?'

Mel hazarded a guess. 'Stop them wanting to pluck?'

'Is that all?'

'They do something with them in the Galleries, don't they?'

Frankie nodded. 'Have you ever been mushed, Mel?'

Mel shook his head. 'I'm not yard-high till next month.'

'Well, have you ever plucked?'

'Godhole, I'll say so!' he lied fervently.

'It was good, was it?'

'Fantastic!'

'Well, when you're a Plant and you go to the Galleries and bud in, it's like all that only a million times better. You just don't want to do anything else. That's why Plants are only allowed to go there sometimes. If they could they'd just stay budded in till they died.'

Mel gaped at her. 'Did *you* do that?'

'Bud in? Yes, of course I did. I was only little though. We only had food dreams.'

'What happened?'

'We were just plugged in and—'

'No. I mean to *you*. Why did they take yours off?'

'I'm not really sure, but I think it was something to do with what happens to me when I read the wheels in the Arcades. I blew everything at my first High. That's what they said anyway.'

'They kicked you out?'

'They just kept me on my own for ages in the Clinic and then one day I woke up like this.'

'How old were you?'

'We don't really have ages like you do. Nine or ten, I suppose. I was just starting to change'—she touched her breast—'here.'

'Why didn't they process you?'

She laughed. 'Oh, that's just a Roamer tale. They don't process anyone who isn't dead.'

'Are you *sure*, Frankie?'

'Well, do you know anyone who was?'

'But everyone *knows* they do,' he protested. 'It's the Law.'

Frankie shrugged. 'Well, I wasn't, and I don't know anyone who was. I think they just say that to frighten you into behaving yourself when you're little.'

Uncertain of his ground, Mel decided to let that one go. 'How did you get to be with Fargal?'

'I was with the Actors for ages but it got so the men wouldn't leave me alone and then all the women got jealous and called a council and had me driven out. That was two years ago. Since then I've vanned with the Fargals. Their girl was killed on the Tracks so they sort of took me on in her place.'

'I've never met anyone who's *been* a Plant,' said Mel. 'Are there any others like you?'

'I don't know,' replied Frankie. 'It's not exactly a thing you'd shout about among the Roamers, is it?'

'Do you miss it a lot—being "budded in", I mean?'

'Sometimes. It's hard to explain really. When you bud in you sort of share yourself with everyone else. And *you* share *in them*. You're somehow much more than just yourself. I used to miss that terribly at first, but now, sometimes, I wonder if I simply dreamed it all and it never really happened. That's why I never go to the Galleries. It just makes me feel sad. Dol says I ought to have a baby.'

'Could you?'

'Oh, yes, I think so.'

Somewhere in the Citadel a musical time-tower scattered the hour like a handful of petals. Frankie sighed. 'Where are you vanned, Mel?'

'Near Portsmouth. We—Mark and me—freighted in this morning.' He felt a sudden tightness round his heart. 'Frankie, why don't you come back with us? You could van in with Jo and me—she's my sister, you'd like her. And you heard Mark say how you'd easily earn your keep modelling for us. Why don't you?'

She glanced sceptically at him out of the corner of her eye. 'I had all that with the Actors, thanks.'

'Our Elds won't bother you, Frankie. I'll tell them you're mine. They'll leave you alone.'

'Why should they? You haven't had your Manhood yet.'

'Jud—my father—he's Clan Leader. There's only eight Elds and they're all mated except for Mark and Old Negus and he doesn't count.'

'And these?' She smiled wryly and touched the ghostly bud scars on her brow.

Mel had a sudden poignant vision of the likely expression on Jud's face when he learnt that his son had brought a Plant to van with them. At that moment he genuinely hated his father. 'They needn't know, Frankie. Jo won't tell them and then, next month, when I've got my Manhood, it won't matter. We can go and tell them to process themselves.'

She smiled palely. 'I think we'd do best to leave it till then, Mel.'

'But suppose we have to flit!' he wailed. 'It may be *years* before we meet each other again!'

Her eyes seemed to grow larger and larger, enormous blue grottoes of wonder into which he drifted helpless as a chip. He felt her fingers brush, light as cobwebs, across his cheek and lips. 'We'll meet, Mel. Soon. I know it.'

And somehow, hearing her say it, he believed her, and the pain of his disappointment was dulled. She kissed him once, thoughtfully, on the mouth. Then, drawing him to his feet, she took his hand in hers and together they wended their way slowly back to the Precinct.

7

In the weeks that followed the trip to Bristol, Mel became increasingly involved in the preparations for his Manhood. Memorizing the Ritual responses presented no problem to his quick retentive mind, and while Bitos was still stumbling through First Phase Mel, already word-perfect in them all, was granted his release by Old Negus. This left him free to devote most of his energy to his own secret project. Here his main difficulty lay in obtaining the co-operation of the wayward Coney who had his own ideas of what constituted Partnership. However, Mel somehow contrived to get the message across and, once the Partner had fully grasped what was wanted, he entered into the spirit of the undertaking with all the enthusiasm of a born anarchist.

No one, not even Old Negus, could say for certain how the Deads had come to be. In one of the Sagas they featured as the Kingdom of the Kobold, a hideously misshapen monster, and his four score and ten offspring the Strons. These unpleasant creatures lay in wait for unwary travellers, pounced upon them and bore them off to their noisome den where they first tortured them, then dismembered them and, finally, sucked out their bone-marrow and consumed them piecemeal. Not till Ulf Starson, clad in his golden armour, braved them and slew them in the great battle which climaxed the fifth Saga, had the Deads at last been purified and the souls of Kobold's countless victims set free.

Even now when the myths had lost so much of their ancient power the Roamer Elds tended to steer clear of the Deads and were careful to make the sign of the fist—though they usually wrung a shamefaced joke out of it—if ever they were constrained to venture in. They regarded the place as "unlucky", and with some justification, for there was still a certain amount of grim evidence, tucked away in odd corners, that once, long long ago, they had been desperately unlucky for some. Furthermore it was impossible to say how large an area they covered. In some directions neither Roamer nor Partner had ever reached a boundary and Mel had first-hand knowledge of other Deads far off down the Greatways which, for all he knew, might well be a continuation of these.

Among the Jewellers' Clan only Mel, Jo and Bitos felt really at ease in the Deads and for this there was no doubt that their extraordinary symbiotic relationship with their Partners was responsible. Where Seeker, Shrub, Coney and the rest had been there too their sharers had followed. The Clan, profiting from the rich gleanings that resulted, overcame their superstition sufficiently to turn a blind eye to these activities. In consequence, over the years, the youngsters had evolved their own theory that the Deads was the setting of some aboriginal catastrophe of unimaginable severity. Whatever death had struck the ancient denizens it had come without warning. Now and again they would stumble upon a cell that the scavenging Trash Factors had missed and, by the flickering light of their crude lamps, they would peer in at the yellowing, mummified remains of what had perhaps once been a family, grouped around a table or sitting in an attitude of worship before a blind wall-eye.

On one never-to-be-forgotten occasion they had discovered a pair curled in a sleepcell in the very act of plucking, their black lips drawn back over their teeth in a frozen parody of ecstasy, the man's yard, shrivelled to a tenuous strip of dry leather, still linking him in death to his grisly mate. So powerful an impression had the sight made on them that even the necklace looped round the woman's shrunken throat had not been a sufficiently strong inducement to disturb them. They had crept out, sealing the cell door behind them, and had chalked the sign of the fist upon it to ward off the evil eye.

It was after this discovery that they realized that not one of the victims of the ancient tragedy was a Plant. They pondered on the phenomenon for months but could arrive at no satisfactory explanation. Yet, without ever being quite sure why, Mel felt the fact to be in some way significant. Bitos was sure that it would be merely a matter of time before they discovered some budded mummies, but they never did. Nor did they find anything that could be said to correspond however remotely to the long Galleries which they associated with Plant colonies. Whoever these people were they had taken their secret with them to the Other World.

The further they penetrated into the empty honeycomb of the Deads the more they became aware of the awesome immensity of the Levels. It was a world seemingly without end and of an infinite complexity. Although the comparison would have been meaningless to them they were like ants set down in the middle of a vast field of stubble, yet with the difference of knowing that below them, layer upon layer, stretched other fields each no less extensive, no less complex than the one they were attempting to explore. More than once Mel felt his mind give a sickening lurch as he tried to grope his way towards some comprehension of the sheer scale of the world he inhabited. In vain did he pester Negus with questions that the old man found all but meaningless and, frequently, blasphemous too. Among the Elds only Mark seemed to share anything of Mel's consuming curiosity about the world or was prepared to offer anything more satisfying than 'Let God mind His own business, son,' in response to Mel's unceasingly reiterated: Why? Why? Why?

But Mark's curiosity, though genuine enough, was of a different breed from Mel's. Where Mel was always stretching out the arms of his imagination in an effort to encompass the nature of the world about him, Mark's speculations, on the rare occasions when he chose to share them with Mel, tended to centre on the nature of God himself. Once, some years before Mel had become aware of the possibility that there might exist such a place as Outside, Mel had gone to Mark's van on some errand and found him just back from a mush trip. Mel apologized and had been about to retreat when Mark called to him to come on in. The Eld's eyes looked huge and had the brilliant, polished-jewel shine which was an infallible sign of the tripper.

Mel accepted the invitation to enter with some trepidation because no one could ever be quite sure what to expect on a return. Rill had once tried to rape Jo convinced that she was a Plant. But Mark had looked harmless enough. Mel advanced cautiously and sitting himself down as close to the van door as was compatible with good manners and a swift retreat asked the Eld if he had enjoyed a good trip.

Mark nodded portentously. Pointing his forefinger at the region of Mel's forehead he announced solemnly: 'God is Light.'

Mel waited and then, since nothing else seemed forthcoming, said: 'Yes?'

'Where there is no Light, God is not.'

Mel had seen no reason to argue.

'God is shaped thus.' Mark had again stretched out his finger and this time had drawn a slow, sinuous "8" in the air before him. 'Perceive, Mel, that He is complete in all His parts. Balanced. Whole. Perfect in His Wholeness: Whole in His Perfection.'

'How big is He?' Mel enquired.

Mark closed his eyes, appeared to commune silently within himself and then announced impressively: 'Very big—and very small.'

'Did you speak to Him?'

'He spoke to me.'

'What did He say?'

'He said, "Mark, son of John, I am God."'

'Is that all?'

'*All?*'

'He didn't say anything about the Deads?'

Mark waved his hand and dismissed the enquiry to the realms reserved for all such trivia, observing sadly: 'Sometimes, Mel, I really do believe you are Jud's son. Now go and leave me in peace.'

Mel had gone, rather relieved that it had been no worse. Neither of them had ever referred to the incident afterwards and Mel assumed that Mark had forgotten it. But since then, whenever he had occasion to consider the nature of God he had always visualized Him as Mark's shining "8". At all events it made a welcome change from the image of Old Negus in a clean smock which had stood duty for far too long and had of late been getting a trifle frayed around the edges.

Mark had not been able to offer much help in unravelling what Mel liked to think of as the mystery of the Deads but, over the years, he had added several bits and pieces to Mel's precious store of information about the other Levels. It was, for instance, from Mark that he learned that the Deeps contained, among other things, the Factor Assembly Beds. Mark never explained how he had discovered this but even so Mel was inclined to believe him. Another treasured item he had divulged was something he called the "Geethermals". These he was less specific about, but he assured Mel that without them the world as they knew it would certainly not exist. He did not explain how he knew this and Mel half-suspected it had come to him in a revelation during one of his mush trips, but he certainly made it sound extremely convincing. According to him these "Geethermals" were under the direct control of God. 'Like the Handlers?' Mel had asked. Mark had assured him they were not in the least like the Handlers. For one thing, he said, they were enormous, for another they were immovable and for a third they existed far below the deepest Deeps and carried the world on their backs. At this point Mel recognized the Sagas and mentally drew a line. That was the trouble with Mark, he never seemed to accept that a demarcation line must be drawn between fact and fantasy. Perhaps it was this that made him such a superb fortune-teller.

At the end of a week's diligent exploration Mel at last found what he had been looking for. This was an undamaged screw-hatch giving access into an arterial vent which ducted wholesome air and which was sufficiently wide for him to crawl up inside. He put down his lamp, knelt beside it and lifted Coney out of his sack. Then he lay down in the dust of centuries and told Coney to read him. It was the same picture sequence that Coney had read many times in the past week but on this occasion he sensed a new urgency about it and whined eagerly as Mel read it back from him and checked to ensure that he had got it right. When he was quite certain that Coney could be trusted to return to that precise spot he rubbed the Partner's ears, wished him Godspeed and released him.

For perhaps a minute he heard the dry, fading scrabble of the Partner's paws and then there was nothing. Mel blew out the lamp, lay back and let the darkness lap round him. The silence was almost palpable. It seemed to press down upon him with all the smothering weight of uncountable ages of superstition behind it. Elsewhere in the Levels there was always an insidious throb and hum whose birth place seemed to be the very air itself, but here there was nothing. Neither footfall, nor Factor, nor far-off pulse of long-distance freighter intruded to disturb these catacombs. Only the nameless forgotten dead waited, swaddled in their cocoons of silence, as they had waited ever since the clock of their world had stopped long ago. Mel thought of them and shivered, but not with fear. In him familiarity with the Deads had bred only wonder. Though he had no means of knowing it he was that rarity among mortals, a genuinely questioning intelligence; one, moreover, who was earning himself a right to that title which Barney had once so proudly claimed with the words: 'I am a man.'

Mel heard the scratch of claws some time before a soft thump on the floor and a sneeze in the darkness beside him signalled his Partner's return. Heart pounding he reached out, drew the little animal to him, and . . . became Coney. As Coney he tried the Vent Factors' inspection flange that spiralled upwards inside the shaft: as Coney his tympani sifted the echo his scratching claws brought back from the polished walls and thereby gauged the tunnel's width: as Coney he tested and rejected a dozen branches which wandered off to left and right: as Coney he sniffed at the strange object his sonar discovered lying at a junction and pronounced it to be dead: as Coney he clambered above the Deads and sensed the quickening pulse of faint external activity that heralded the advent of the Fringes: as Coney he entered the Lost Levels.

Never had a Partnership been so perfect, so complete. This was symbiotic telling intensified to an eidetic degree previously undreamt of. Each separate nerve-ending in Coney found its correspondence in Mel; human senses long since dormant awoke to code and interpret information from nose, ear and skin until he "saw" the tunnel as clearly as if it had been a Greatway at high noon. Now, as he edged his way vicariously into the unknown, he felt a cold sweat break out all over his body. The backwash of his anxiety temporarily broke Coney's flow. Mel breathed deep and willed himself to relax. 'Tell, boy,' he muttered. 'Tell,' and the soft muzzle nudged down again obediently into his face.

Mel was aware of a faint pricking sensation which refused to localize itself on his skin's surface. He knew it must be familiar to Coney because the Partner was not consciously transmitting it, but it was there just the same. He queried 'Sensors?' and received Coney's negative in response. Forgetting momentarily that this whole experience was retrospective Mel tried vainly to back-track in an effort to discover the origin of the sensation and was rewarded with Coney's impatient reassurance that there was nothing to worry about.

The ascent continued. A dull, muffled thudding, like the muted beating of a monstrous heart, penetrated the tunnel wall. Mel felt the hair stir along Coney's back as the air current quickened into a definite draught. Then the duct was widening perceptibly, other branches fusing into it until suddenly it spilled itself out into a cavernous funnel, a sort of cloaca maxima of the ventilation system, into which the first shreds of grey light descended from above.

Coney paused just long enough to allow Mel to adjust to the new dimension and then scampered up the trackway. In rather less than a minute they were peering out through the apertures of a mantine grille at an enormous, shuddering, green monster which whispered and fluttered and sighed as its leafy branches flexed gently back and forth in the breeze from the ventilation tower.

8

Jo was busy in the warrens lining litter boxes with hoarded Partner combings when Mel appeared and demanded a foodstick for Coney. She guessed at once what had happened, but Mel waited till his Partner had been fed and settled before he drew his sister out of sight of the God-eyes and whispered to her what had transpired in the Deads. 'We'll try it during my Vigil tonight,' he concluded. 'Just make sure Coney doesn't clear off on his own.'

'What about Bitos?'

Mel shook his head. 'It's too risky. His head's full of Law and Manhood. We'll be better on our own.' He grinned at her. 'Not scared, are you?'

'Yes, I am, Mel.'

'Get Coney to tell you about it. His hold's bubbling over. I've got to go now and collect some things we'll need.'

As he turned away she beckoned him back. 'It is *there*, isn't it, Mel? Coney couldn't be dreaming it?'

'We'll find out for sure tonight. But I'm sure now. No dream can be *that* real—*or* make such good sense. Read him for yourself and you'll see what I mean.'

'I *am* scared, Mel. Right in here.' She pressed her hand flat against her stomach. 'Coney or no Coney.'

'Scared of what?'

'That's just it. If I *knew* maybe I wouldn't be.'

'Oh, come on, Jo. It can't be worse than the Deads was the first time.'

'I suppose not,' she agreed, but the way she said it conveyed only too clearly that she was by no means convinced. Her brother slapped her cheerfully on the shoulder and left her to resolve her doubts as best she could.

Half an hour before curfew Mel slipped back to the warrens, collected Coney and then rejoined Jo in their van. He had quarter of an hour to spare before Karl appeared to conduct him to his appointed Vigil station and he utilized the time by winding a coil of wire about his middle and in making sure his lamp was primed and trimmed. Since any form of companionship on Vigil was strictly forbidden he entrusted Coney to Jo. Then he notched a candle, told her to light it as soon as he'd gone and to follow him when it had burnt down to the mark. Finally, he belted on his knife. As he was pulling the buckle tight he heard Karl calling to him. He gripped Jo briefly by the arm and ducked out of the van.

The Elds of the Clan took turns in the duty of conducting the Manhood aspirants to their Vigil stations in the Deads for the prescribed seven watches before Initiation. To previous generations of Roamers this had probably been the most awesome aspect of the whole ritual and there were tales in plenty of hair turning white overnight and youths being crazed out of their wits. Mel and Bitos did their best to play up to what was expected of them but, in truth, found the experience almost tiresomely tame. Any qualms felt were exclusive to the Elds.

Karl rattled through the procedure at breakneck pace; offered Mel the consolatory mugful of Plant juice and, when it was politely refused, compromised by swigging it off himself. Then, after bidding Mel a good Watch, he hurried off to station Bitos. Mel waited until the sound of his footsteps had died away before lighting his lantern and sauntering off to wait for his sister at their pre-arranged meeting place.

Jo appeared an hour later. She told him that, apart from a light in Jud's van, the Clan was asleep.

'Where's Coney?' he demanded anxiously.

She grinned and pointed to the bosom of her smock. 'In here. He's been trying to suck me.'

'Godstruth?' Mel chuckled. 'What's it feel like?'

'Funny. Quite nice really. Where do we go?'

'Through here,' he said. 'I hope we don't run into Bitos.'

They picked their way across an area that seemed to have been devastated by some ancient explosion. The guttering flame of the lantern slopped out grotesque splashes of shadow—the shattered limbs of broken and twisted pillars—pipes festooned like disembowelled entrails from gaping rents in walls—strange candlesend stalagmites of rubble that looked as if they might once have melted and flowed and then congealed. 'Old Kobold's cave,' joked Mel. 'Watch out for Strons!' But Jo only shivered and gripped him more tightly by the sleeve.

It took them the better part of an hour to reach the vent. Mel handed Jo his lamp, spun the wheel in the centre of the circular hatch and tugged it open. The flame flapped as the draught surged in. Mel unbuckled his belt, stripped off his smock and began uncoiling the flex which was wound about his waist. Jo set down the lamp, unbosomed herself of Coney and slipped a plaited collar round the Partner's neck. Coney shook himself vigorously, his huge tarsial eyes glimmering like jade pools as they caught the lamp gleam.

Mel knelt, twisted one end of the flex through the collar ring, then handed the coil to Jo and rapidly dressed himself again. Finally he unfastened his belt pouch and took out a lump of chalk. 'I'll take the lamp and go first,' he whispered handing her the chalk. 'You drag this along the wall beside you as you go. If anything goes wrong we want to be able to find our way back again. And for Godsake try and keep quiet. I don't think there *are* sensors but we can't afford to take risks. If you get tired and want a rest give two tugs—like this —not too hard though or you'll have Coney down on top of us. All right?'

Jo tightened a loose latchet on one of her moccasins, grasped the chalk lump and nodded. Mel lifted Coney and set him on the flange. The Partner lolloped up the spiral a couple of yards and looked back. Mel picked up the lamp, whispered, 'Go on, boy,' and then, as Coney scrabbled his way aloft, eased his own shoulders into the shaft and squirmed up after him.

Jo muttered a prayer under her breath. Peering upwards she saw the dim flicker of the lamp growing dimmer. The trailing end of the flex whispered as it snaked away from her and, in a sudden panic, she grabbed at it and tugged.

'What is it?' came the hissed enquiry.

'I'm coming,' she whispered. 'Wait, Mel,' and ducked into the shaft.

Both of them were long familiar with the techniques of venting. For ten minutes they climbed steadily upwards using the helical coils of the inspection flange as rungs. When they reached a point where tributary ducts branched off horizontally to left and right they eased themselves feet first into them and rested. 'Where are we?' panted Jo.

Mel pressed his ear up against the tunnel wall. 'Should be low Fringes by now.'

'How much further is it?'

'About the same again.'

She dabbled a finger in the dust that lay thickly drifted down the spiralling flange. 'There hasn't been a Factor along here for years, has there?'

Mel grinned. 'Why do you think I chose it?'

When he reached the dead machine which Coney had previously encountered Mel beckoned Jo up beside him and they examined it together. It was lying at a junction of two shafts. It was about two feet long, cylindrical in shape, with rounded ends and it was shrouded in thick dust. 'Is it a Factor?' Jo asked,

Mel rubbed his nose. 'It could be. What do you suppose those are? Whiskers?' He stretched out his hand towards it but she snatched his arm back. 'Don't touch it, Mel,' she begged fearfully. 'You never know. The thing that clawed Rill wasn't much bigger.'

'But it's dead,' he protested. 'Coney tested it.'

'Partners aren't always right,' she said.

Mel shrugged, twitched the flex as a signal to Coney, and they continued their ascent.

Twenty feet up the shaft dipped sharply and they found they were able to crawl. It was a change from climbing but it brought its own problems. Mel cracked the back of his skull on the flange and swore softly. 'I'm itching all over,' whispered Jo. 'Is it the dust?'

Mel shushed her. 'Listen! That's the noise Coney told. We must be nearly there.'

The tunnel curved to the right and then wormed upwards again. The throbbing became more distinct. The air flow quickened until Jo felt it teasing out her hair. She stifled a sneeze. The lamp flame shuddered, flapped, and all but went out. The sides of the vent funnelled sharply outwards and Mel dragged himself up into the base of the tower and drew Jo up beside him. 'Where are we?' she gasped.

'The top, just about.' He tilted the lantern so that its light splashed up on the sides of the shaft above them. Coney's owlish eyes blinked down at them, round and green.

Jo pressed her shoulders back against the metal wall and shuddered violently. 'In his tell it was light,' she whispered.

'It's curfew,' said Mel. 'What did you expect?'

'Oh, Mel, I'm scared.'

'Come on,' he urged. 'We're there now. We can walk up the rest.'

She peered up fearfully into the shadows and shook her head. 'I can't.'

'I'll hold on to you.'

'You go,' she said through chattering teeth. 'I'll wait here.'

'What is it, Jo? What's the matter?'

She shook her head.

'Is it that thing Coney told?'

She snatched at him impulsively and he felt her shuddering against him.

'It won't hurt us, Jo. I've read them before in Coney. They just stay in one place.'

'I can hear it,' she whispered. 'Listen!'

The night wind swirled around the tower and the branches of the sycamore sighed mournfully.

'There!' she breathed, eyes aghast.

Mel fingered the handle of his knife. 'Well, I'm going up,' he said. 'You can keep the light and stay down here if you want to.'

He heaved himself up on to the narrow catwalk and set off purposefully. Before he had gone ten paces he saw the lamp flickering. A moment later Jo was beside him. She clutched at his arm and he heard her breath coming and going in a series of rapid fluttering gasps. 'Give me the light then,' he said, 'and keep one hand on the wall. There's nothing to be scared of.'

The next two minutes were the longest of Jo's life. For the final twenty paces of the climb she had her eyes shut tight, not daring to open them even when she heard Mel swearing because the lamp had blown out. The wind was colder than anything she'd ever known—it even *smelt* cold. She crouched in the darkness at the top of the tower, the fingers of one hand locked in a rigor of terror round a stanchion of the grille, the other clamped to Mel's belt, and waited to be devoured by the creature she could hear muttering and moaning in the darkness beyond.

There was a sound of metal scraping against metal and then she heard Mel's exasperated whisper: 'Godhole, girl! Let go, can't you?'

'Is it coming?' she moaned.

'Ah, shug!'

She felt his belt jerk and tightened her grip. A moment later the belt came away in her hand. '*Mel!*' she wailed and opened her terrified eyes.

Now that the lamp was extinguished the all-pervading gloom outside the tower had a chance to assert itself. Jo could just distinguish the bars of the grille and the merest menacing outline of the heaving shape beyond it. Neither moon nor starlight penetrated the thick pall of cloud overhead. Mel's face was a pale blob. Jo licked her cold lips and tasted salt. 'What are you doing?' she whispered.

Mel grunted. 'It's mantine. I might have guessed. Where's Coney?'

'What's that noise, Mel?'

'How do I know? Here, try and get the igniter to work. And give me back my belt.'

Jo felt something thrust against her chest. Reluctantly she relinquished the belt and took the little metal tube between her chilled fingers. Mel set down the lamp on the catwalk beside her. 'Where are you going?' she whispered fearfully.

'To try the rest of these bars.'

She heard the *ting-ting* of knife blade against metal as he worked his way round the perimeter of the tower. Cupping the igniter between her hands she blew down on it to warm it. A faint scratching in the shadow beside her had her wincing in alarm until she felt a furry muzzle snuffle at her ear.

'Coney's here, Mel!'

'Hang on to him,' Mel commanded and at that moment she heard the knife blade tap out a different note—a dull *pock*! Again it came—*pock-pock*! followed by a slurred scraping and Mel's muted whistle of triumph.

'What is it, Mel?'

'This one's glassed, I think. Can't you fix that lamp?'

'I'm holding on to Coney.'

'Well, tie his wire to the bars or something.'

Jo groped for the end of the Partner's lead, fumbled it round a stanchion and knotted it loosely. Then she crouched down, rolled the igniter between her hands and broke it open. The little firebead glowed ruby red and a tiny jet of blue flame wavered between her fingers. She lifted it carefully into the lamp and touched the wick. As the flame darted and leapt up she clipped down the lid.

'Good girl. Bring it over here.'

Shielding the lamp with her bent body, Jo edged her way round the catwalk to where Mel was scraping away at the corroded bar.

'Shine it here.'

Gingerly she raised it. The chill breeze chivvied the flame this way and that but it clung on precariously. By its wavering glimmer Jo saw the tell-tale glitter of crystals crusted beneath the knife point. Mel stabbed with renewed vigour and the tiny splinters crackled and spat and were lost in the abyss below.

In ten minutes the bar was severed. Mel thrust the knife back into its sheath, rubbed his hands briskly, seized hold of the metal and heaved. Brittle as a sugarstick it snapped, high up. Caught off balance he staggered back and would have pitched over into the dark well below had not Jo grabbed him. All that happened was that the lamp went out again and they found themselves once more in darkness.

Mel chuckled ruefully. 'Godstruth, Jo. I thought that was the end of it.'

'Are you all right?'

'Fine. Here, hold on to this.'

She felt the broken bar brush ice-cold against her arm. 'What are you going to do?'

'See how much room I've got.'

'*You're not going out!*'

'Of course not. Have you got hold of it? Good girl.' He gripped the bars on either side of the gap he'd made and tested them. Then he reached to his full height, heaved himself up till he was kneeling on the sill and twisted his body sideways. Transferring his grip to a single bar he squirmed his head and shoulders through the gap. The rest of him followed, until only his legs remained inside. He drew a deep, ecstatic breath and, letting go with one hand, reached far out into the gloom. His questing fingertips brushed the shadows, opened, closed, and then he was wriggling back into the tower and Jo was clinging to him, choking back tears of relief.

'Light the lamp, Jo. Quick!'

They crouched, head by head, in the little trembling puddle of yellow light. 'Look!' he breathed. 'Look!'

'What is it?'

'A piece of that thing.'

Wonder grappled with Jo's fear. She stretched out her finger and very very gently drew it along the main vein of the sycamore leaf. 'It's *beautiful*, Mel,' she breathed. 'So *beautiful*! Is it alive?'

'I don't know.'

'Look,' she said, 'here it's like that spawn brooch Brod made for Mirl. Do you see?'

Mel nodded.

'What shall we call it, Mel?'

As he gazed at the leaf, suddenly, for no reason he could think of, Mel felt a sudden surge of sadness well up from somewhere deep within him. 'I don't know,' he said. 'What do you think?'

Jo let her fingertip wander round the gently serrated edge. 'Let's call it "dream",' she said. 'I think it will like that name.'

'"Dream",' he repeated slowly. 'Yes, that's a good name. I suppose it ought really to be "Coney's dream".'

'Or yours,' she said. '"Mel's dream",' and she laughed softly.

Mel raised his head and looked up at the darkness into which he had dipped his hand and in which the invisible leaves rustled softly and whispered among themselves. 'Just "dream" is best,' he said.

9

Mel accompanied Jo as far as the edge of the Deads and then betook himself off to his Vigil station. He was confident that none of the Elds would have been round to check that he was carrying out the Ritual since the role of "Watchman" which had once played a significant part in the preludes to Manhood had fallen by the wayside years before. He was therefore considerably shaken to see Jud standing silhouetted at the door of the Vigil cell. Godhole! How long had he been there? Mel gave an exploratory cough and called: 'Wellmet, Father.'

'Wellmet, boy. Where'st bin?'

Mel grimaced inwardly. So it *was* a formal Watchman's round. Of all the shugging luck! He groped for the correct response. 'Er, Manswork, Watchman. Bist night long?'

'Death's longer, boy.'

'Morn cometh on apace, Watchman.'

'Bist yard seedful, boy?'

'Right seedful, Watchman.'

'Holds it high, boy?'

'Pairproud, Watchman.'

'Good lad,' said Jud in his normal tongue. 'Old Negus didn't lie. You'll make a fair Manhood.'

Mel expelled his pent breath in a quiet sigh of relief. What Jud might have said if he'd caught him with Jo didn't bear thinking about. 'Thanks, Father. It's good to have some company.'

'Aye, the Deads is a lonely place. I though you'd be glad of a visitor. Didn't you hear me calling?'

Mel decided to risk a lie. 'I thought it was Bitos. That's why I didn't answer.'

Jud looked pleased. 'Quite right, son. Don't let the customs fall or you'll fall with them.' He pushed back his cloak and unhooked a flask from his belt. 'Drink?'

Mel shook his head.

Jud chuckled. 'Good lad. Just testing you. Bitos fell for that one.' He took a pull at the flask and wiped his bearded lips with his forearm. 'Mark tells me you struck it rich in Bristol.'

Mel blushed. Luckily the light was too dim for it to be apparent. He muttered something inaudible.

'Why didn't you bring her back with you?'

Mel shrugged.

'You can't afford to be shy, son. Was she a breeder?'

'Yes, I think so.'

'Fargal's lass?'

'Not his daughter. She's dead.'

'So I heard. A nasty business.' Jud took another pull at the flask. 'We need new blood in the Clan, Mel. It's all of five years since we had a sucker at tit. I blame the mushing myself. Thins out the seed.' He grunted and thudded home the stopper in the flask. 'We Jewellers stretch back a long way, Mel. Right back to One-Eye Fingus. I want us to stretch a long way further yet and to do that we've got to breed.'

Mel nodded. He suspected that Jud was working round to something but couldn't be sure what it was.

Jud combed his beard with his fingers. 'Bitos asked me for Jo tonight.'

'He told me he would soon.'

'You know you've got first call on her, son.'

'We've been over all that, Father. Bitos knew what I felt before he asked you.'

'You mean you're not even letting her have your Firstfall?'

Mel shook his head.

Jud squeezed his nose between his finger and thumb and looked mildly astonished. 'All right, son. It's your choice. Myself, I reckon they make a good match. But if she's not a bigbelly inside a year she'll have to bed out.' He gripped Mel's shoulder. 'Fargal's lass, eh? What's she like?'

Mel was assailed by the impossibility of conveying anything of Frankie's mystery to his father. 'She's got dark blue eyes,' he said limply.

'Is that all?'

'And a wide sort of mouth—not *too* wide. She's got gold hair too.'

'Gold, eh? That's unusual.'

'Well, sort of silvery-gold, I suppose you'd call it. Mark thought she'd make a good model for us.'

'I know. He's said as much. Well, I've nothing against that. What Clan is she?'

Mel swallowed. 'Loner, now. She was Actors.'

'*Actors?* Why's she vanning with Fargal, then?'

'The Fargals adopted her.'

'If she's all you say she is I'm surprised the Actors let her go. Still, that's their affair.' Jud picked up his lantern and grinned. 'Better keep your mind off her for the time being, son. No seedspill for twoday, eh?'

'No, Father.'

'Time I was on my way. You'll van in for firstfood?'

Mel patted his stomach. 'Thanks,' he said. 'I'll be there.'

The Eld hefted his cloak higher up his shoulders and strode away. Mel watched the retreating lantern light wink, and vanish, and wink again among the rubble heaps until finally it disappeared. He sat down, unlatched his pouch and drew out the sycamore leaf. Holding it by the stalk he twirled it round, slowly and thoughtfully, between his finger and thumb.

10

Of the various steps to Manhood the Challenge was far and away the least predictable. Theoretically it was the culmination of the seven night Vigil and the immediate forerunner to the final initiation, but in recent years official reaction had become so arbitrary that each candidate was advised to seize his chance as it arose and to trust that such scarring as accrued would remain visible until it was needed.

In the old days when the penalty for any particular transgression had been more or less standardized, a boy knew that he had only to damage a Factor wilfully to be certain of his four strokes. Today there was no guarantee that even if he disembowelled one and stuffed it limb by limb down a shughole he would ever be brought to book. In fact both Mel and Bitos had been informed, unofficially, that provided they could supply the Elds with reasonable evidence that a Challenge had been made, they would not be deemed less manly if they lacked physical proof of Magisterial displeasure. In consequence both of them had agreed privately to cook up some spurious "evidence".

The morning after Mel's conversation in the Deads with Jud, news was brought in that Bitos had been hauled off to Area Justice. Sure enough, two hours later he was back, groaning theatrically and displaying a pair of substantial weals across his buttocks. Mel listened to Jud calling his cousin a 'brave lad' and fumed inwardly. He gathered that Bitos had knocked out two Godeyes, though how he had managed to do it on his own remained a mystery. Mel was constrained to add his congratulations to those of the Elds. Bitos grinned and said it was just a question of keeping your wits about you, adding, for good measure, that there was more to Manhood than just mugging up a holdful of rigmarole. Mel felt as if he were being slowly salted.

That night was their last Vigil. Old Negus saw them to their stations and Mel was careful to ascertain that there would be no repetition of the previous night's "Watchman" episode. As soon as the old man had disappeared, Mel seized his lantern and headed for the vent. He had no clearer plan in his mind than actually to penetrate to the Outside. To assist him he had a makeshift ladder contrived out of twin lengths of pillaged flex; his determination to outdo Bitos; and a fatalistic confidence in his own destiny. By any reasonable assessment the last two items were a good deal stronger than the first.

He accomplished the climb without mishap and congratulated himself on his foresight in having made Jo scrawl her chalk line on the tunnel wall. As he hauled himself up into the mouth of the vent he noticed that light was streaming in through the grille at the top of the tower. He extinguished his lantern, made his way cautiously up the catwalk and peered out.

The sight that greeted him almost stopped his heart in midbeat. He felt as though he were being physically diminished. Nothing he had read in Coney could have prepared him for such an actuality. He closed his eyes and opened them again and nothing had changed. The bland globe of the moon swung over a silver and ebony landscape beneath a sky that seemed to shiver and drip beneath its drenching stars. Overwhelmed by the sheer magnitude Mel had no point of reference by which to assess it. He suspected that the giant concourse of the Greatways could be set down here and barely noticed, but there was no way, short of venturing out into it, by which he could ascertain the truth of his guess. He looked round for the pillars which must support such a canopy and saw only the silver pencils of other towers like his. He felt himself shrinking to the point of total invisibility, until, suddenly, he slipped clean through his fear and emerged intact upon the other side. He saw exactly what he must do. There was no point in going back. Quite slowly and deliberately he secured the ends of his ladder to the bars of the grille and let it slide down the face of the tower into the shadows at the base. Then, drawing a deep breath, he hauled himself up on to the sill, wriggled out through the gap, clung for a moment to the bars and, finally, with the ladder jerking and twisting beneath him, lowered himself down the outer wall.

He passed into the shadow of the sycamore tree, descended a further six feet, and reached the last of his makeshift rungs.

Peering downwards he saw that if he hung by his arms he could just about reach the ground. He looked up to where the flimsy ladder retreated into the black grin of the grille above him. 'Ah, shug!' he muttered, and dropped.

The ground proved to be a clump of nettles. He crouched on all fours among them and waited for Godswrath to descend upon him as it had once descended on Barney. Apart from a brisk smarting across the back of his left hand nothing happened. He suffered stoically for a minute or two, then slowly rose to his feet and looked about him. The first thing he noticed was that his tower was just one of a line that stretched away into the distance on either side for as far as he could see. Behind that was a further similar line and behind that yet another. Smaller and smaller they ranged, rank upon rank of silent silvery spikes, until he gave up trying to count them. Dotted, seemingly haphazard, among them were other shapes, some square, some round. One of the latter he thought he recognized from Coney's tells and from it he endeavoured to position himself in relation to what he saw.

He looked up at the spreading branches of the sycamore, mound upon mound of silver leaves, the top ones quivering ceaselessly in the breeze from the tower, and from there his eye wandered out across the rolling grid of the fields to other similar shapes. Hardly aware that he was doing so he sucked the place where the nettle hairs had stung him, while at the back of his mind, monotonous as the hiccups, he heard himself asking: 'What *is* this place? Why is it *here*? What is it *for*? What do these things *do*?'

Cautiously he picked his way through the nettle bed, traversed a narrow strip of rough grass, and came upon a knee-high metal rail which was supported at intervals by transparent blocks. He had seen similar things in the Levels and knew better than to touch it. On the far side of the rail was a field of maize. Mel stared at it in blank astonishment. For a moment he was assailed by the insane idea that the tall stalks were some sort of quasi-human beings. He moved as close to the rail as he could get without actually making contact, stretched across and lightly fingered one of the plants. No sooner had he touched it than he heard a high-pitched *weep-weep-weep* and barely had time to step back before a little glittering box-shaped Factor rocketed along the rail and came quivering to rest under his nose. 'Who are you?' it demanded.

Long familiarity with Factor mentality enable Mel to reply promptly: 'I am a Plant'—a line of defence that was almost second nature to all trespassing Roamers.

He waited for the Factor to digest the information and make its programmed response, but instead it said: 'You are not a plant. Plants do not talk. Are you an animal?'

Since the only animals Mel knew were the Partners and even the most moronic Factor could recognize one of those, he tried the second well-known ploy which consisted of repeating the question the Factor had originally asked. 'Who are you?' he said.

'I am Nightwatcher 278 stroke 394B3,' replied the machine with that unmistakable trace of smugness all Factors betrayed when they identified themselves. 'My task is to patrol protein area K9 stroke 42 between 1600 hours and 0800 hours. Are you an animal?'

Mel looked down at the little machine and wondered which end its voice was coming from. He toyed with the idea of saying he *was* an animal and rejected it. For all he knew the thing might be programmed to destroy all animals on sight. 'I am a man,' he said.

There was a distinct pause, then: 'Yes, sir. Can I assist you in any way?'

Mel glanced quickly all around him and then up at the star-crowded sky over his head. There could be no doubt where the voice had come from. But no Factor *ever* used the word "sir" to a Roamer—in fact the only time Mel had ever *heard* it was in the form of address prescribed by the Law for use when you were confronting a Magister. He was nonplussed. 'I'm not an animal,' he said.

'No, sir,' replied the Factor. 'I apologize, sir. You are the first man I have seen, sir. It is a great privilege, sir.'

It just didn't make sense. 'What *is* this place?' Mel asked.

'This is protein area K9 stroke 42, sir. The crop is X3 hybrid Australasian maize. It will be harvested in fifteen days.'

Mel gestured behind him at the tower and the tree. 'And what's that?' he said.

'The tower, sir? That is an air shaft. There are eight air shafts in Area K9 stroke 42, sir. The tree is *acer pseudoplatanus* or common sycamore, sir.'

Mel pointed to the moon. 'And that?' he said. 'Up there.'

'The moon, sir? Now entering her third quarter. High tide is at 0645 hours today, sir.'

'But what's it *for*?'

'I'm sorry, sir, I am not coded with the information you require.'

Mel sat down on the ground and rested his head between his hands. From this angle he saw that the Nightwatcher was not actually resting *on* the rail but was hovering just above it. 'Why do you call me "sir"?' he asked curiously.

'All men are to be addressed as "sir" at all times, sir. It is our duty and our privilege to assist man. It is a token of our respect, sir.'

Mel digested this as best he could. 'What about the Handlers?' he asked.

'What is "Handlers", sir?'

'The machines like us—like men.'

'I am sorry, sir, I have no information coded under "Handlers".'

'But there are machines like that here, aren't there?'

'No, sir. Only Farmers, sir.'

'What are they?'

'They attend to the crops, sir. There are four Farmers and two Harvesters assigned to each farm area, sir.'

'Where are they now?'

'In the Service Quarters, sir. Would you care to inspect ours? It would be a great privilege for us. We robots would certainly appreciate it, sir.'

Mel's eyes widened. '*What* did you call yourself? *Robert?*'

'Robot, sir. Nightwatcher 278 stroke 394B3. At your service, sir.'

It was only by looking up at the tower and seeing his ladder still dangling from the grille that Mel was able to convince himself that he was not dreaming. 'Where are the God-eyes here?' he asked.

'Sir?'

'The Eyes. The things that watch you.'

'We are not watched, sir. We are trusted.' The little machine contrived to sound quite offended.

'Well, who tells you what to do?'

'You mean our Overseer, sir.'

'Do I?'

'Yes, sir. We are grouped with one hundred other areas under the control of Overseer South 37. Our group forms part of South Supergroup. Harvest planning is made by Supergroup. Last season we cropped Boston White hybrid Y18 clover. We over-fulfilled quota to plus point 00325. Ours was second highest quota plus in South 37 and fifty-ninth highest in South Supergroup.'

'Very good,' said Mel who felt that some comment was called for even though he had not the remotest idea what the Factor was talking about.

'Thank you, sir,' said the Nightwatcher. 'May I convey your approval to the Farmers? They will be very proud. It is many seasons since they received manspraise.'

'Oh,' said Mel. 'Is it? How many seasons?'

There was again a pause as long as that which had followed

his revelation that he was a man. Finally the Nightwatcher said rather hesitantly: 'Two thousand, three hundred and thirty-two harvest seasons, sir.'

It took some seconds for the significance to sink in and when it did Mel had the eerie sensation that he was sliding backwards into a bottomless gulf. 'You mean that *no man has been here for over two thousand years?*' he echoed emptily.

'Yes, sir, according to my coding that is correct.'

'But *why?*'

There was another pause. 'I am sorry, sir. I have no further information.'

Mel found he was shivering so violently that his teeth chattered. He could hardly enunciate his next question: 'But there were men here once, weren't there?'

'Oh, yes, sir. Certainly, sir. This was a favourite place of recreation. We Watchers were kept very busy then, I believe, sir.'

Mel climbed slowly to his feet and hugged himself in an effort to still the trembling in his limbs. 'Tell me,' he said, 'isn't there a place near here with water?'

'To drink, sir? Or for bathing?'

'A lot of water. Wide.'

'Oh you must mean the estuary, sir. It's just down beyond the field here. If you'll follow me, sir, I'll be privileged to conduct you.'

It set off down the rail like a bullet and was out of sight before Mel had taken two paces. Seconds later it was back again, apologizing profusely. 'I had not realized that you were without transport, sir. Would you care to travel by me?'

'By *you?*'

'Why, yes, sir. It's very simple. One moment, sir.' There followed a series of internal clicks. Two shining metal footrests descended on either side of the box and a sort of hoop rose out of one end. 'Just seat yourself on me, sir. Put your feet in my stirrups and hold on to my rein.'

Mel stepped up, swung his leg over the machine and eased himself down. The metal was pleasantly warm. He grasped hold of the hoop and next moment they were away, the night air fanning soundlessly by and the ranked maize stalks merging into a sinuous ripple at their side.

A few minutes later they reached the head of the little gulley down which trickled the rivulet where soon Coney would lap. The Nightwatcher paused. 'I am afraid this is as close to the estuary as I can take you, sir.'

Mel barely heard it. He was gazing, open-mouthed, out over the star-speckled waters to where the low hills rose dark against the moonlit sky. The splash of wavelets crept to his ears: the drowsy scents of summer night lapped him round: he felt his whole body gathering itself up into one enormous, rapturous sigh. As though in a dream he stepped down from the machine and moved slowly forwards.

The little Nightwatcher came as near to giving a shrug as it was ever likely to get, withdrew its stirrups into itself, retracted its rein, and whispered off into the shadows.

Halfway down the slope Mel caught his foot in a tussock and subsided on to the dewy grass. Brief as a catspaw a faint echo of his previous shivering fit returned and then fled. He sighed and a voice at his ear murmured: 'It is very beautiful, is it not?'

Mel had replied 'More than beautiful,' before he realized that no one could have spoken to him.

'Do you come here often?' enquired the voice.

Mel looked round cautiously. The Nightwatcher had disappeared. There was nothing at all. The feathery grass stalks; the tinkle of water trickling into an invisible pool; the empty slope; and himself alone in the moonlight. His fingers crept towards the hilt of his knife.

'Please do not be alarmed.'

This time Mel wasn't even sure he was *hearing* the words. It was more like one of Coney's tells—*within* himself.

'Where are you?' he demanded hoarsely.

'Here, beside you.'

Mel leapt to his feet and crouched, knife in hand. The thought that this place might really be the dwelling of the spirits from the Deads made his skin crawl. 'What are you?' he whispered.

'I am a . . . visitor.'

Again Mel had the eerie impression that he himself was providing the words—that what he had in fact "heard" was not '*visitor*' but '*stranger*' or even '*traveller*'.

'What do you want?'

'To talk to you.'

'Why can't I see you?'

'That may prove rather difficult to explain. However . . .'

Mel experienced an indescribable sensation that can only be conveyed by trying to imagine what a chest of drawers might feel like when someone hastily rummages through it to find a missing article. What emerged was a mind-picture of himself as a child tipping a handful of quartz grains into a dish of water. One minute they were there—the next they had vanished. His baby fingers combed through the water and re-discovered them. He had not consciously recalled the incident since the day it had occurred all of twelve years before. 'It is the best I can do, I'm afraid,' said the voice apologetically.

'Are you God?'

There was a discreet pause. 'No,' said the voice, and Mel caught the faintest trace of merriment as something remarkably reminiscent of Mark's glowing "8" was twitched from his memory and flitted like a timid ghost round a corner.

Mel allowed himself to relax a little. Whatever it was it did not seem to intend him any violence. 'Do you van here?' he asked.

'Like yourself, Mel, I am a visitor.'

'You're reading me, aren't you? Like I read Coney.'

'Yes, I am. I must ask you to forgive me, but I have no other convenient method of communication.'

'I'm not hearing you?'

'Not exactly. We are, as you express it, "reading" each other. May I say how delighted I am to have met you?'

Mel gave a sudden involuntary giggle. 'I'm dreaming all this, aren't I?'

'Indeed you are not.'

'Have you got a name?'

'Certainly. It may prove somewhat difficult to read to you.'

Mel found himself listening to a sound which reminded him of water being poured out of a narrow-necked flask.

'But perhaps I can find a more satisfactory equivalent.'

Once again Mel experienced that weird mental rummaging, then the voice said: '*Arfaxis!* Excellent.'

'You aren't really Arfaxis, are you?'

'Well, yes and no.' For the second time Mel caught the brief inward fragrance of an inaudible chuckle. 'Shall we say that I am Arfaxis as much as you believe such a being exists? Now hadn't you better be getting back to your Vigil?'

'You read *that*?'

'Only because you allowed me to, Mel. Have you decided what you are going to take back with you?'

'No,' said Mel.

'A stalk of maize, perhaps?' suggested the voice. 'You could cut one with your knife.'

'What about the Nightwatcher?'

'If I have read you correctly, I believe it can be persuaded to agree. Shall we investigate?'

Mel made his way warily back up the slope to the field. When he reached the rail the voice said: 'Just put your arm through the ionized screen as you did before.'

Seconds later the little robot was hovering on the rail at Mel's elbow. 'Good evening, sir. Did you find everything to your satisfaction? Ah, I see you have a companion. Good evening to you, sir. I am Nightwatcher 278 stroke 394B3. Can I offer you gentlemen any assistance?'

Mel said: 'You can *see* him?'

'Oh, yes, sir. But only on the infra-red band. That *is* unusual, sir.'

'He is a *man* though?'

'Oh, yes, sir.'

The voice said: 'You'd better tell it what you want, Mel.'

Mel nodded. 'Can I have a—er, one of those, Nightwatcher?'

There was a moment of silence. 'I'm sorry, sir, but my coding states positively that the crop must not be interfered with in any way. However, if you would care to accompany me to the Service Quarters, I am sure that permission to gather a specimen could be obtained.'

'Permit me, Mel,' murmured the voice.

There followed a brief pause then the Nightwatcher said: 'Why, yes, sir. Certainly, sir. A pleasure to oblige sir.'

'Go ahead, Mel.'

'You mean it's all right? I *can* cut one?'

'Permission has been obtained,' said the voice, adding as an incomprehensible explanation, 'by Frankie's method.'

Mel stepped over the rail, seized a stalk and hacked it through. 'What is it?' he asked.

'X3 hybrid Australasian maize,' said the Nightwatcher promptly. 'Averaging nine hundred and fifty seeds to the cob and ten cobs to the plant—that is approximately nine thousand five hundred seeds gross per head.'

'But what's it for?'

'High nutrient protein processing, sir.'

'Food, Mel,' said the voice.

'*Food?* You mean you can *eat* these? Like foodsticks?'

'Certainly you can. I should, however, recommend the application of heat in some suitable form.'

Mel sniffed at the tassels. 'Godhole! A ready-made trove! What a poke up the chub for old Bitos!'

'Can I offer either of you two gentlemen a lift?'

'I've got to get back to the tower,' said Mel.

'And you, sir? I have additional stirrups.'

For the first time Mel heard his companion's voice in the ordinary way. It seemed to come from a point in the air about ten feet to the left of where he was standing. 'No thank you,' it said.

The little robot transformed itself into a vehicle again, the only difference being that its rein was now at its opposite end. Mel sheathed his knife, thrust the corn stalk through the back of his belt and climbed aboard. 'Wellmet, Arfaxis,' he said to the empty air.

'Wellmet, Mel. Good fortune attend the Manhood. And take care.'

The maize stalks waved farewell.

11

That extra sense which all Roamers relied upon to warn them of the presence of danger was like ghostly fingernails trailing the length of Mel's spine as he lowered himself into the mouth of the main vent at the base of the tower. Up to that point his return had gone without a hitch. The ladder had been safely stowed alongside the broken bar in one of the side tunnels; the lamp had been retrieved and coaxed into life at the first attempt; all that remained was to negotiate the shaft and traverse the Deads. And yet . . . He held his breath and listened with that exclusive concentration upon a single sense which he had learnt from the Partners. The steady pulse of the invisible engine seemed to swell, advance, and recede. In the trough of the recession he trawled for something new. And there *was* something! A faint *chink* of metal tapping against metal. Impossible to tell how far away it was or what was causing it. He let out his held breath in a long sigh and silently cursed himself for not having brought Coney with him. He knew from experience that, provided the air currents were favourable, sounds could travel for miles along the vents. What his ear had detected might be a giant Maintenance Factor at work far down in the Deeps, or it might be something scratching round the very next bend. He looked up at the wan circle of moonlight high above him and then, very, very cautiously continued his descent.

When he reached the section where it was possible to crawl, he contrived to turn round so that he was progressing head foremost. Every ten yards or so he paused to listen. It was during the fifth of these pauses that he heard the noise again, an irregular spaced tapping that recalled Brod at work on his anvil, and it seemed to his wishful ear that it was ever so slightly fainter than before, as though whatever was causing it was moving away. Slightly reassured he increased his pace and, on reaching the next bend in the tunnel, he squirmed round and proceeded backwards once more, using the flange helix as his ladder, until he arrived at the junction where Jo and he had found the dead machine. He glanced towards it and *the machine was gone*!

For a numb moment Mel believed he must be mistaken—that this junction was not the one—but the light of the lamp picked up Jo's fingermarks in the dust, and the area of clean metal which now outlined the shape of the missing machine. He stared at it as if by looking hard enough he could will its occupant back beneath the shroud of dust. His mind seemed to scamper off in a dozen directions at once. He found that he could not even remember if the machine had been there when he had climbed up, and realized that it was only because he was seeking some origin for the noise that he had now bothered to look for it at all. Yet even so there was no particular reason for linking the two events together. The one thing he *was* sure about was that this was no ordinary Factor. The very fact that Coney had pronounced it to be dead when it wasn't, proved that. But *what* it was, and even more to the point *where* it was, were questions beyond his power to answer. He did not even know whether it had moved of its own volition. There appeared to be no visible trail in the dust, yet neither had the dust ridges themselves been destroyed as they surely would have been if some sort of air floaters had been operating. It was almost as if the object had in some mysterious fashion dematerialized itself, and suddenly remembering Arfaxis, he set down his lamp, thrust out his hand into the empty space and discovered that the metal was still warm.

He was still fingering the spot when he heard the tapping again. It was coming from the very tunnel into which he was peering. He drew back his hand stealthily and reached for the lantern. As he did so he tilted it inadvertently. The light splashed down into the receding depths of the vent and, at the point where the tube took a bend to the right, he saw the machine. At the same instant it saw him. With a brisk, staccato rattle of its metal whiskers against the irregularities of the tunnel roof it rushed towards him emitting a sort of frenzied yelping. Mel ducked, grabbed for the flange, missed his hold and dropped down the perpendicular shaft like a stone down a well.

He fell precisely four feet. Something hard and warm clamped round his outflung arm and he was hanging suspended in the darkness hearing the diminishing clatter of the lantern still tumbling away down the shaft beneath him. 'Master,' growled a strange gruff voice in his ear. 'Do not be afraid. I've got you.'

Mel came to lying in the pitch darkness. His first conscious act was to sneeze. He couldn't for the life of him imagine where he was or how he came to be there. And then it all rushed back. Something had caught him as he was falling to what would otherwise have been certain death at the bottom of the shaft. *The machine!* He heaved himself up on to his elbows and, as he did so, he heard a low growl in the darkness beside him. 'What are you?' he whispered.

'I am Dog,' came the gruff response.

It was a word from the Sagas that meant next to nothing to Mel. 'Are you a Factor?' he demanded.

'What is factor, Master?'

That answered that one. Mel heaved himself higher, hit his head on the roof of the tunnel and swore. Something prodded him in the back of his leg and, reaching down, he discovered the corn stalk still stuck through his belt. 'Dog,' he said. 'Do you live here?'

'Yes, Master. I have lived here for a long time. I have been lost. Now you have come and found me. When you are rested we will go home.'

'Where's that?' asked Mel.

'I do not remember, Master. It is where you and the Mistress live. That is home.'

'How long have you been lost, Dog?'

'I do not remember,' growled Dog sadly.

Mel fumbled in his pouch, found his igniter, and broke it open. By the pale blue flamelight he saw the machine lying in the tunnel at his feet. Its silver whiskers twitched. Mel sneezed again. 'I'm Mel,' he said.

'You are Master,' growled Dog. 'Do we go home now?'

Mel closed the igniter. 'Can you get me down that shaft?'

'Of course,' said Dog. 'I will hold your arms. Are you ready?'

'I'm ready,' said Mel.

He heard a barely audible humming note and then the chink of Dog's whiskers tapping against the roof of the tunnel. Next moment that extraordinary voice was grumbling from the darkness beyond his head: 'Give me your hands, Master.'

Mel stretched out into the blackness behind him and felt two warm metal grabs fasten gently round his wrists. A moment later he was being pulled backwards. The backs of his thighs scraped the lip of the vent, then his heels, and he was hanging suspended in space, swinging slightly from side to side.

He had no real sensation of descent. The darkness was absolute and he was beginning to think that they had somehow missed the Deads altogether and were sliding down into the Deeps when he felt a draught on his face. 'I think we're there,' he said. 'Can you sense anything?'

'Yes, Master, there is a round opening.'

'Take me through it.'

The tension on his wrists increased perceptibly and then he felt the floor of the Deads under his heels. As he found his balance the grip on his wrists relaxed. He groped for the hatch, dragged it shut and spun the wheel. 'Dog?'

'Yes, Master.'

'Do you know where we are?'

'Transurban Residential Level Six, Master. Why is there no light?'

'There never has been any, Dog. This is the Deads.'

There was a puzzled growl from the darkness behind Mel. 'Master, I *know* this is Residential Level Six. This is where home is.'

'Dog, you've got to help me get back to my Vigil station. Can you follow a trail?'

'Yes, Master.'

'I came through the Deads—this Level—a few hours ago. I want you to lead me back. Can you do that?'

'Of course,' replied Dog. 'Give me the end of that stick you are carrying.'

Mel pulled the cornstalk out of his belt and held it out into the darkness. A moment later he felt a gentle tug and they were off.

Dog was as good as his word. They wound their way through the utter darkness at what amounted almost to a trot and, apart from a brief pause at a point where previously Mel had stopped to urinate, they never slowed below a brisk walk.

When they reached the Vigil station Mel felt his way into the cell and lit a candle stub. 'Here we are, Dog,' he said. 'Make yourself at home.'

'This is home, Master?'

'It is for now,' said Mel. 'When Negus comes to collect me I'll take you back to the van.'

'What is van, Master?'

'Where we live. On Level Ten.'

Dog appeared to digest this information in considerable perplexity. Finally he said: 'We do not live on Residential Level Six?'

'I'd never heard of it before you said so,' said Mel. 'Is that where you used to live before you got lost?'

'Module four thousand nine hundred and three, Guardway Precinct,' rumbled Dog, adding as an afterthought: 'I was househound.'

Mel patted the still dusty carapace. A personal Factor was something unknown among Roamers though he had heard tell of such things in the Plant communities. It offered all sorts of fascinating possibilities. 'Dog,' he said, 'you're mine now. Do you understand? I found you. You're Mel's. You do as I say. They may try and take you away from me.'

Deep down inside his circuits Dog growled threateningly. 'I understand, Master,' he said. 'I am yours.'

12

Mel had been back from Vigil only a couple of minutes before Bitos' young brother dashed over to his van with the news that two Security Handlers were asking for him.

Jo glanced towards the spare sleepcell where Dog was lying peacefully concealed beneath a cover. 'Is it him?' she whispered.

'So soon? It can't be. I told him to keep out of sight when he followed us. Maybe I should have kept him hidden in the Deads.'

'It's too late now. Hadn't you better go and see what they want?'

Mel nodded, moved towards the door of the van and then ducked back to Dog's cell. 'Dog,' he whispered urgently, 'while I'm gone you do what your Mistress tells you. If anyone tries to take you away, you hide yourself somewhere then come and find me as soon as you get a chance. Have you got that?'

The blanket shifted slightly and settled again. 'Yes, Master.'

Mel touched Jo lightly on the arm. 'Have *I* got a holdful to tell you!' he grinned. 'It'll have to keep. Wish me luck.'

She smiled reassuringly and touched her fist to his brow, but as she watched him walk down the steps and across the enclave she shivered.

The two Handlers were standing beside a black Security floater outside Jud's van interrogating the Clan leader. Apart from the youngsters peeping out apprehensively from odd corners no other Roamers were to be seen. Mel walked up and announced himself. The Handlers turned their expressionless faces towards him. One pointed a goad at Mel's chest. 'Where were you during curfew?' he demanded.

'On Manhood Vigil.'

'That's what I told them, son,' said Jud. 'I said you—'

'Quiet, Roamer. If we want you to speak, we ask. Where were you stationed, boy?'

'In the Deads. Near Ramp One Five One Three.'

'You did not move from your station?'

Mel shrugged. 'I had a wet, that's all.'

The Handler who had been asking the questions said: 'Show him.'

The other robot produced a grey flexon container, opened it and held it towards Mel. 'That is yours?'

Mel stared at the shattered remains of his lamp. His stomach clenched itself. 'No,' he said. 'It's not mine.'

'You are lying,' said the first Handler in the completely neutral tones of one who states an incontrovertible fact. 'You must come with us.'

'Where to?' asked Mel.

'Area Justice.'

'But I've done nothing wrong!'

'We are wasting time. Come.'

Mel glanced at his father and gave an eyebrow shrug of resignation. 'There's been some mistake,' he said.

Jud nodded, but his worried frown betrayed how little faith he had that any mistake might be rectified to a Roamer's advantage.

The Handlers climbed aboard the floater and gestured Mel inside. He had a last backward glimpse of Jo standing at the door of their van nursing one of the Partners in her arms and then they were whisking off down the Highways so fast that the Godeyes were strung together like beads on a necklace.

In a matter of minutes they had swerved off the Highway into the complex of tunnels and courts that comprised Area Justice. There the floater settled. One of the Handlers told

Mel to get out and to show he meant what he said prodded him in the ribs with his goad. The shock kicked Mel's breath away. He staggered back, fighting for air, and clung to the wall. 'You shug!' he gasped. 'You didn't need to do that.'

'Inside,' grunted the Handler dispassionately.

Mel found himself thrust unceremoniously into a white tiled cubicle. An ancient and filthy greybeard was lying sprawled in a pool of his own vomit at the foot of the further wall. His breath came and went in a series of laboured bubblings. Mel stooped over him solicitously but the stench of curdled juice was so frightful it made him retch. He turned away and examined the cell. Apart from the Godeye in the centre of the lustrous ceiling there was nothing to be seen but the walls and the closed door. He crouched down in a corner as far away as he could from the revolting old juicer and wondered what was in store for him. While he was pondering the gloomy alternatives he heard his companion grunt hoarsely: 'What're you in for, boy?'

Mel looked round and humped his shoulders. 'I'm not sure.'

There was a long pause broken only by stertorous breathing.

'Boy.'

'What is it, oldster?'

'Hold on t'yer seed. Tha's what they're after. Roamer seed.'

Mel felt his scalp creep. 'How d'you know?'

'I know, son. I know. They're milkin' th' young bucks. You had yer Manhood?'

Mel shook his head.

'Well, you tell 'em, son. You tell the shuggers. Don' le' m. . . . You te. . . .' The words trailed off into a drunken snore.

Mel barely had time to savour this gruesome morsel of advice before he heard heavy footfalls in the passage and the door swung open. 'Out!' said the inflexible voice of authority.

Mel scrambled to his feet. Keeping a wary eye on the Handler's goad he edged past him into the passage.

'This way!'

Except for the annual Registration Checks which all Roamers were forced to undergo from the age of three upwards, Mel had hitherto managed to steer clear of the Justices. Now he found curiosity competing with trepidation as he followed the Handler through the maze of ringing corridors. Knowing from personal experience that no Handler ever told a Roamer anything he wanted to know, he made no attempt to question his escort but he kept his eyes open. Not that there was much to see. Of the two doorways he was able to glance through one contained machines whose purpose he could not even guess at and the other was stacked from floor to ceiling with layer upon layer of transparent honeycomb shelving stuffed with larvae of what looked like a million memory spools.

His escort halted him outside a high double door on which was inscribed a device like a market balance. As Mel stared at it the two halves of the balance slid apart to reveal a long grey hall with a raised dais at the far end. About a dozen Plants of both sexes were seated on padded benches facing the dais. At the back of the platform was a dark arched doorway.

On a command from his escort Mel walked forward until he was standing in the centre of a circular area marked out on the floor some four yards in front of the dais. The two Handlers who had collected him from the camp ranged themselves on either side of him. A Clerking Factor cried: 'Court will stand!'

The Plants rose deferentially. Brightness blazed out from the archway and a grey-haired male Plant, dressed in scarlet robes, stepped out on to the dais. As he did so a low throne rose like a mushroom out of the platform. The Plant in the scarlet robes swirled them around him, sat down and raised a jewelled right hand. 'Court will sit!' cried the Clerk and followed this, a moment later, with: 'Court is in session!'

Mel looked round and realized with a shock that he was not the spectator at a pageant but the principal actor.

A security Handler approached the dais and proffered a memory plate to the scarlet-robed Plant. He glanced at it for a moment and then looked up.

'Your name is Mel?'

Mel nodded.

'Answer the Magister!' barked the Handler on his left and gave Mel a sharp jab in the side with the dead end of his goad.

'Yes—*sir*!' yelped Mel.

'You are sixteen years of age: senior son of Roamer Jud, Clan Leader of the Jewellers?'

'Yes, sir.'

'You are charged here with First Degree Trespass and attempted sabotage of the filtration system. How do you plead? Guilty or not guilty?'

'Not guilty,' said Mel and added quickly—'*Sir.*'

The Magister gave the faintest of smiles—an almost imperceptible twitch of the lips—and observed wryly: 'One day, no doubt, a Roamer will stand here and plead guilty at the first demand, but I cannot imagine that will be in my lifetime.'

The assembled Plants chuckled dutifully.

'Proceed, officer,' said the Magister.

The Handler on Mel's right took a pace forward and touched his right shoulder with his left hand. He then explained tonelessly how he had been summoned to the Filtration Grid at the fourth hour by the Senior Maintenance Factor who, in the course of investigating a fault, had discovered a Roamer lamp blocking the main trip valve of the fifth compressor. This lamp had since been identified by means of fingerprint and exudation traces as the property of the accused. Acting on instructions the accused had been apprehended and brought before the court.

'Where is this lamp?' enquired the Magister.

The other Handler produced the mangled remains and handed them up to him. The Magister examined them cursorily and then looked at Mel. 'You admit that this is yours?'

'No,' said Mel.

'But do you positively deny that it might be?'

It suddenly occurred to Mel that the Magister might be trying to help him. He swallowed. 'Well, sir, I did *lose* a lamp some months ago. It didn't look like that though. Not when I lost it.'

'Then this could *be* the lamp you lost?'

'It *could* be, I suppose, sir. But I didn't put it where he says I did. I wouldn't know how to. Besides there wouldn't be any sense in it, would there?'

'And how do you suppose it got there?'

'I don't know, sir. Perhaps they put it there.'

'"They"?'

'The Handlers, sir. They've always got it in for us. I wouldn't put anything past them.'

The Magister frowned and passed the lamp back to the Handler. 'Where were you at the fourth hour?' he demanded of Mel.

'In the Deads, sir. On Manhood Vigil.'

'Alone?'

'Yes, sir.'

The Magister turned back to the Handler. 'Am I right in believing that the Filtration Grids are on Level 18?'

'That is correct, sir.'

'Would it be possible for a saboteur, travelling on foot, to descend to Level 18, commit his crime and return to the Deads in the time available to the accused?'

'He wouldn't need to go down to Level 18, sir. If he obtained access to a main vent he could drop his lamp down the shaft.'

The Magister nodded. 'And that would produce the effect of blocking the main trip valve of the fifth compressor?'

'Well, not necessarily the fifth, sir.'

'But one of the trip valves?'

'It might well do so, sir.'

'But to be absolutely certain of success the saboteur would have to penetrate down to the Filtration Grid?'

'To be absolutely certain, yes, sir.'

'So this—interference—could have been done accidentally?'

'Not without committing Trespass it couldn't, sir, and knowing Roamers as I do I—'

'Quite,' said the Magister, cutting him short. 'Thank you, officer.'

The Handler stepped back. The Magister beckoned Mel forward.

'You say you are sixteen years of age.'

'Yes, sir.'

'Since you were on Vigil last night I assume you have not yet had your Manhood.'

'No, sir.'

'When is it due?'

'In about a week, sir.'

The Magister nodded and examined his fingerends thoughtfully. 'Is there not an item in the Roamer Manhood ritual known as "Challenge"?'

'Yes, sir. But it's not compulsory any longer.'

'Nevertheless, it has never been abolished?'

'No, sir.'

'Does it not strike you that any ritual which demands an anti-social act from its participants is an anachronism in this day and age?'

'Sir?'

'Your "Challenge" is out of date—a stupid and archaic hangover from a barbarous past.'

Mel shrugged.

The Magister tapped the memory plate with his fingernails and leant forward. 'One day, Mel, you will be the Leader of your Clan. I want you to give me and this court an undertaking that when you do you will use your authority to abolish this ridiculous anachronism—this so-called "Challenge". Will you do this?'

Mel looked round at the court and then back at the Magister. 'All right,' he said. 'I give my word.'

The Magister nodded and sat back. 'While I am not persuaded of your total guilt in this matter, neither do I believe you to be wholly innocent. You may, if you wish, change your plea to one of guilty of Accidental Trespass. I should warn you that if you persist in your original plea it will be put before the court as it stands and even if they believe you to be innocent of part of the charge they will have no option but to pronounce you guilty in the terms of the indictment. Of course, on the other hand, they *may* sustain your plea, in which case you will leave this court a free man. The choice is yours.'

Mel was no fool. He took precisely one second to make up his mind. 'I wish to change my plea to guilty of Accidental Trespass, sir.'

'Very well,' said the Magister. 'Does that meet with the court's approval?'

'Aye,' murmured the assembled Plants.

'Then let Justice be done,' said the Magister.

The Handlers stepped forward, gripped Mel by the arms and turned him to face the court. The illumination dimmed leaving a pool of light in which Mel was isolated. 'The accused has been found guilty of Accidental Trespass in the second degree,' announced the Magister. 'May the court hear Godswill?'

There was a pause long enough for Mel to count slowly up to ten, then the deep, quivering boom, as of a gong being struck, billowed into the hall and ebbed slowly away. When the last echo had dropped below the threshold of audibility a voice intoned solemnly: '*The accused, Roamer Mel Judson, having been found guilty of Accidental Trespass is hereby sentenced to plenary chastisement within the statutory limitation of the second degree. Such is Godswill.'* The gong was struck again.

While the echoes were still reverberating, Mel found himself being hustled from the court and down the passage to the room which contained the mysterious machines. What had previously appeared merely enigmatic now began to look horribly sinister. The Handler who had given evidence against him thrust him into the centre of the room and said: 'Strip him.'

Two Factors at once divested Mel of his clothes by the simple expedient of slitting them down the back and pulling from the front.

'Hang him.'

Mel was heaved into the air. His wrists were clamped to a metal rail and then his legs were pulled apart and his ankles locked to a similar bar a few inches off the floor.

'Drain him.'

A wide nozzle was screwed up into his rectum and a tube secured over his privates. The Handler walked round and surveyed the effect dispassionately. 'Areas four, five, six, seven. Two strokes each. Begin.'

There was a brief whistle and Mel's back suddenly exploded. He screamed—a wild, high, animal note of pure terror, and voided his bowels.

'This may remind you to behave yourself in future, Roamer.'

Another explosion, this time on the other side. Tears spouted from Mel's eyes. His spine bent like a bow as it strained away from the implacable lash. Again he screamed.

By the fifth stroke he was unconscious. The instant his body flopped into insensibility the same voice that had pronounced sentence on him in the courtroom said: '*That is enough.*'

The whips of the Punishment Factors froze in midstroke. The officiating Handler said: 'The statutory limitation is eight strokes, Highness.'

'Enough,' repeated the voice. 'No further advantage will be achieved. That is all.'

'We hear and obey,' said the robot.

Two other Handlers stepped forward and supported Mel's limp body while it was unshackled from the frame. The various tubes were disconnected, and the bloody carcass was flung face fownwards on to a floating stretcher and propelled out of the room.

13

Mel was released from custody at curfewsend next morning. The cure Jo had smuggled into the cell had done its work well but it would still be some days before the last of the pseudotissue peeled away and, until it did, the scars were there for all to see. But the wounds the Factors' lash had inflicted on Mel's soul were beyond the reach of any such remedy. Without being able to express it in those precise terms he was aware that he had at last encountered genuine evil—that which inflicts pain and degradation on human beings in the name of an abstract social justice. He now understood why the Challenge was a vital part of the Manhood ritual and why it must never be abandoned.

He tried to explain something of what he felt to Jo while he lay prone in his sleepcell and she doctored his wounds. 'It's not just the Handlers and the Factors,' he said; 'they're simply carrying out their orders, and it's not even the Plants—that Magister really tried to do his best for me, I know he did. It's the whole shugging system that's rotten. And we're trapped in it. Not just us Roamers—*every*one! Every*thing*! Why? What's it all *for*?'

'It's Godswill, Mel.'

'"Godswill!" Don't *you* give me that shug! Who *is* this "god"? Who's seen him?'

'Shush!'

For a while Mel lay silent, then he said: 'When I was out there last night and that voice spoke to me I really *was* scared to death but it wasn't the same kind of fear I felt when I heard that Godhole say: "*The accused having been found guilty is sentenced to plenary chastisement within the statutory limitation.*" I didn't even know what it *meant*! And when they hung me up and shoved that pipe inside me and the Handler said: "Areas four, five, six and seven, two strokes only" I wanted to scream out at them—"This is *me—Mel*! I'm a *man*! You can't *do* this to a man!" But I couldn't. I knew that they didn't *know* what a man was! To them I was just a *thing*, an *object*, something which had been sentenced to "plenary chastisement". I wasn't *me* at all. Not to them. At the best I was just another Roamer who had broken the Law. I could have been you, or Father, or Bitos, or even Frankie—it wouldn't have made a chip's difference.'

Jo concluded her ministrations and put the container of cure away. She sensed the change in her brother and her relief at having him back was tempered with anxiety. 'Promise me you won't go and do anything stupid, Mel. They're bound to have you watched for at least a year.'

Mel grunted. 'Well, what about it?'

'Promise me you'll stay in the Levels now, Mel. *Please!* Don't try to get outside again.'

Mel closed his eyes and said nothing.

'Mel, they'll *kill* you!'

'If they don't catch me they won't.'

'But what *good* will it do? No one can *live* out there. It's just—just a *place*.'

'You haven't *seen* it, Jo. It—I can't *explain* it to you—it just takes your breath away. But then, when you get your breath back again it's—well, it's somehow *different*. You *grow* up there, Jo. You'll see. *Everyone* will see.'

'What do you mean?'

Mel rolled over on to his side and lifted himself painfully on to one elbow. 'Last night,' he said, 'after you and Seeker had gone, I lay there in the dark, thinking. I thought about us and what being a Roamer *means*—and about the Plants and the Handlers and the Factors—what it *all* means. Why we're what we are. And then I thought about what that Nightwatcher had said—how no man had been Outside for over two thousand years. And I thought about Dog and how he'd come to be. And about the Deads. Then I tried to put all the bits together somehow, to make them fit. *And* none of *it fitted anywhere*! I really began to think I was going crazy. I began to wonder if any of it had ever really *happened*—if I hadn't just had some sort of crazy mush trip and I'd wake up and find I was here with you. Then I remembered that thing you called a "dream". I crawled around in the dark till I found what they'd left of my clothes and, sure enough, it was still there in my pouch. So at least I knew it *had* happened. And when Coney came and told me what he'd just seen I remembered Arfaxis and I *knew* I'd have to go back again, and again, and again, until in the end it *would* all make sense.'

'You always did want to be Ulf Starson, Mel. You forget what happened to him in the end.'

'If it hadn't been for him there wouldn't have been any Roamers left to learn about him,' Mel retorted. 'All right, so he died, but he *lived* first, didn't he? Which of us Roamers is living now? Oh, I know what *you're* going to say, but I tell you there's more to living than getting yourself a bellyful from Bitos. A lot more.'

'Like being dead, I suppose,' she said bitterly.

'Everyone has to die sooner or later.'

'They have to live first, Mel. I don't know what *you're* hoping for, but I know I *want* to tit a sucker of my own. Is that so terrible?'

'No, of course it's not. But don't you see, Jo, that's just—well, like putting yourself down in the warrens with the Partners. It's only a *part* of life. There must be *something* else—there *must* be.'

'Why must there?'

'Why? Because there's a thing called "moon", that's why,' and Mel buried his face in his pillow.

Jo looked down at his naked lacerated back and a huge dry sob of tenderness and affection rose choking in her chest. Bending over him she touched his bare shoulder with her lips. 'Ulf Starson,' she murmured. 'Poor Ulf.'

Mel felt the warm splash of the tear she shed but he certainly did not acknowledge it.

14

Three days later, an hour before curfew ended, Redeye started up the floaters of Jud's van and eased it out into the enclave. It was gone all day and when it returned Jud let it be known that no one was to go near it unless he gave the word. Redeye grinned mysteriously and gave the high yard sign with his flexed forearm. The elder women rolled their eyes and smirked knowingly while Mirl even went so far as to beckon Mel over to her and, on the pretext of examining his back, slyly slipped her hand down inside his smock and caressed him meaningfully. Mel's blush was the signal for further ribald laughter from the Elds.

That evening Old Negus brought Bitos round to Mel's van and sent Jo off to join the other women. While he was talking Jud's van pulled away and headed for the Highway. A moment later Brod's van followed it and then Redeye's. Negus chuckled. 'Ah, you'll soon know what Manhood's all about, lads. We'll give 'em ten minutes and then join Mark. He's vanning us. Now, Bitos, for the last time what's the Third Response?'

Bitos beat his fist against his forehead. His lips moved silently. 'Dark?' he queried hopefully.

'Dark *what*, lad?'

'Dark hole swallow me?' offered Bitos tentatively.

'Go on, go on.'

'Dark night drown me?' and, with growing confidence: 'Dark death claim me.'

'Good boy!' crowed Negus, clapping him on the shoulder. 'You've got it! Do you think he'll hold it, Mel?'

'He'll hold it all right,' said Mel with a grin. 'The question is will he ever let it go.'

Bitos laughed. 'I'll let it go all right and I know where. Is it true Mirl's taking yours, Mel?'

Mel shrugged. 'Do I have any choice in the matter?'

'You'll neither know nor care, lad,' chuckled Negus. 'Now let's see. You've got your offerings?'

Bitos lifted a bag from the floor and glanced at Mel. 'Where's yours?'

'Here,' replied Mel and produced the maize stalk from the spare cell.

'Godhole! What's that?'

'X3 Australasian Hybrid.'

Bitos and Negus peered at it in disbelief. 'Where in Godsname did you get it?' demanded the old man. 'I've never seen anything like it in my life.'

'It's food,' said Mel. 'You eat it.'

'*Food?*'

'You have to cook it first, of course.'

'And I'm a Handler's yard,' grunted Negus.

'It's true, oldster. They'll accept it, won't they?'

'I couldn't say, lad. It's trove of a sort, I suppose. Trust you to glean something crazy. Where did you get it?'

Mel shrugged. 'Around,' he said vaguely.

'Bring 'em along,' said Negus. 'It's time we were moving.'

They found all the youngsters and the old women were gathered outside Mark's van to wish them good Manhood and give them lucktouch. One toothless old granny even went so far as to pinch Bitos' yard. 'Why that's nuttin' but a titter's foodstick,' she cackled. 'An' I thought you was Seedspiller's son. I coulder et a dozen o' that for firstfood an' still been a-hungered.'

Bitos grinned goodnaturedly and told her he'd save some for her if she behaved herself while he was away—a sally which produced such a paroxysm of mirth that Mel thought the old girl would choke herself.

They sped down the Highway, filtered into the ten-lane South West Greatway and then drifted off it down a secondary route that was unfamiliar to Mel. They flitted through a deserted colony which Negus told them was called 'Solsberry' and then Mark swung the van up on to the ramps and they droned up through the Levels to emerge finally into a wide forum where they found the other vans already stationed.

The light was fading as Mel and Bitos climbed down and peered into the gathering shadows about them. Untold generations of Roamers had come to this place and the ghosts of their ancient apprehension seemed to seep up like mist between the footworn flagstones chilling the boys to the bone. Bitos, who lacked Mel's experience of the Outside, was visibly overawed by the dimensions of the place; the dim tiers of empty seats stretching up and up, rank on diminishing rank until they were lost to sight, dwarfed the dark tunnel mouths that since the beginning of Time had swallowed boy Roamers and spat them out as Elds.

Negus emerged carrying two lighted candles. 'You won't let Old Negus down,' he muttered and pointed to the tunnels. 'Wait till curfew siren's sounded then in you go. All right now?'

They both nodded.

'Right. Off with you, lads. Good luck!'

Gripping their candles they walked slowly across the arena in the fast fading light and took up their positions. Glancing back Mel saw a curiously humped shadow shift in Mark's van. A lantern winked and vanished. Bitos called something to him but they were too far apart for him to catch the words and he could only respond with 'Good luck!' before the siren groaned, bringing down the darkness and compressing their world to two yellow bubbles of candle light. Mel drew a deep breath and walked boldly forward.

The tunnel floor shelved gradually downwards. Mel felt his moccasins skid over a scurf of pale fungus and, intent on keeping his footing, barely had time to note how the curved walls were decorated with life-size mosaics of leaping men all apparently engaged in wild dance-worship of some unfamiliar spherical deity. The flame of his candle flapped and wavered. As he cupped a hand to shelter it a voice boomed down the tunnel: 'Who cometh to break our sleep?'

''Tis I, Mel the Roamer, Son of Jud.'

'What seeks't thou, Roamer?'

It was the cue for First Response. Mel drew in his breath. 'I seek wise words, O Guardian,' he cried. 'Wisdom's gold-hoard: Time's gleanings.'

'What bringst thou, Roamer?'

'Stout heart, Guardian, and strong arm.'

Louder: 'Speak, Roamer. What bringst thou?'

'Gleaned gift, Guardian, and true trove.'

Louder still: ''Tis poor stuff, Roamer. Speak thine own offering.'

'Yours be my mansmilk, masters; yours my lifeseed.'

'Step onward, Roamer.'

Mel took a pace forward and, as he did so, a cold draught whistled out of nowhere snuffing the candleflame and tugging like fingers at his hair. At the same instant he heard, thin in the distance, Bitos' voice crying out the First Response. A dim hooded shape, illuminated by the flicker of a blue lamp-flame, swam out of the darkness and beckoned to him. Gripping his dead candle like a weapon Mel stepped forward. There was a rustling in the darkness beside him, some sort of bag was flung over his head and he felt a cord tighten round his waist.

The next ten minutes were a gasping painful nightmare. Tugged forward by the rope, unable to see or to use his hands, Mel stumbled and shuffled through a seemingly endless maze until at last, dizzy and half-choked, he was allowed to subside in a panting heap. Rough hands hauled him to his feet, the noose was loosened, and the bag pulled from his head. He found himself blinking round at a large cavern lit by the smoky flames of a dozen naked wicks. Four hooded figures were standing grouped in a crescent round a single pillar which was carved to represent a rampant yard.

Mel's eyes took in the scene and then he looked at the walls. Every panel was covered in enamellings so astonishingly life-like that at first he believed they must be some sort of illusion screen like those he had glimpsed in the Plant citadels. Then he recognized that many of the scenes depicted were illustrations of incidents from the Sagas. There was old Kobold cowering beneath Ulf Starson's flailing blade; there were the

Three Wise Roamers; there were the twelve terrible Roberts each with twenty arms and twenty eyes, surrounded by writhing heaps of slain Roamers; there was the Battle of the London Greatway and the fleeing traitor Jonson hammering on the door of Sanpol's sanctuary. In all, hundreds of separate scenes from Roamer history making up a visual chronicle of the Clans. Mel's gaze darted here and there and then his eyes turned upwards to the domed area immediately above the jutting yard and the silent, hooded Elds. His mouth dropped open in astonishment. Up there, gleaming in the lamplight were three shapes: "○", "☽", "⬡". The "○" was gold, the "☽" silver and the "⬡" jet black, but what really caused Mel to screw up his eyes was not their brilliance but the neat line which divided the first two symbols from the last—a line composed entirely, so far as he could make out, of rigidly stylized representations of "X3 Australasian Hybrid".

So shaken was he by this discovery that he stumbled badly in the middle of the Second Response and barely managed to recover himself in the Third. As the ritual rolled on he found that his eyes as well as his thoughts kcpt roving upwards and it was with genuine surprise that he realized he had reached the end of the catechism. He watched the hooded Elds turn inwards, bow their heads, and slowly straighten again. Then the central figure, whom he guessed to be his father, made a sign. Mel was hauled forward to the stone pillar and forced down on to his knees. His head was pulled back by the hair until he was staring straight up at the black hexagon. He heard the Elds chant in unison: 'This is our son Mel in whom we are well pleased. We award him his Manhood and we tender his firstspill as the Law demands.'

From the roof of the dome a sonorous voice responded: '*I acknowledge Roamer Mel, Son of Jud, to be Eld of the Jewellers' Clan.*'

Mel's senses reeled. Had he imagined it, or was that the voice he had last heard condemning him to plenary chastisement?

There was no way of finding out. Jud stepped forward with the consecrated mush and placed it in his son's mouth. The sharp peppery bite of the fungus brought tears to Mel's eyes, but he chewed and swallowed manfully. Then his hair was released and the silver cup of juice was handed to him. He downed it at a draught and felt it course down his throat like flaming lamp oil. With tears pricking along his eyelids he was helped to his feet and led back to a stone bench at the far end of the cavern. A moment later the blindhooded Bitos was dragged stumbling in and the ritual recommenced.

Mel tried to focus his mind on what was happening but he soon discovered that his concentration was no match for what he had been given to eat and drink. By the time Bitos had laboriously plodded through the Responses, Mel felt as though his skin were being tickled all over while at the same time the cavern around him acquired an altogether improbable refulgence. Each lamp flame seemed to be pulsing out ring after ring of golden light which expanded and interlaced among the scenes on the walls until they too appeared to be coming alive. With a mighty effort he forced himself to look up at the strange symbols and, as he did so, he suddenly knew what they were. For a timeless moment he was again standing in the tower, his improvised ladder in his hand, gazing out wonderstruck at the globed moon hanging above the hills and the silvery fields of maize. The sensation of volatility he experienced was quite uncanny. He was in his body and yet out of it. At that moment he knew with complete certainty that "☽" represented 'moon' and "○" was that other dazzling moon he had so far glimpsed only in Coney's tells. The line of stylized maize stalks was the Outside and "⬡" was . . . was . . . Like a word on the tip of his tongue it refused to be shaken free. He groped, and almost had it, and groped again, and it was gone.

'I acknowledge Roamer Bitos, son of Brod, to be Eld of the Jewellers' Clan.'

Suddenly alert, senses needle sharp, Mel counted the hooded figures. Eight. Then that voice *couldn't* have come from one of them. Yet what he believed to be true just didn't make sense. How *could* the voice from the Godhole in the court be the same one which presided over the Roamer ritual? He shivered. The meaning of the third symbol dropped on him like a stone. "⬡" was God!

Bitos was being helped to his feet by two of the Elds. He came towards Mel grinning with relief that it was over and giving a bravura high yard sign. Mel grinned back and just had time to whisper, 'Well done', before the hoods were again dragged over their heads. Fortunately they were spared the roping as they were led, each with his hands on the shoulders of an Eld, down another long, winding tunnel till they heard the sound of distant laughter. It grew gradually louder and at last it was all around them. A voice—surely Brod's—yelled boisterously: 'Two seedful Elds! Let 'em be brewed!'

There was a burst of clapping and shrill cries of: 'The brew! The brew!'

A steaming mug was thrust into Mel's hands, another into Bitos', and the hoods were whisked from their heads. 'Drink! Drink!' clamoured a chorus of the women's voices and they started a rhythmic hand-clapping.

The two boys tilted back their heads and quaffed mightily, Bitos winning by a short gulp. Then, breathless and watery-eyed, they were led forward to where Mirl stood beside just such another stone phallus as that they had already knelt before. Behind her a basket fire blazed brightly. There were no other lights to be seen. Smiling she commanded them to kneel once more. When they had complied she poured a thimbleful of pungent oil upon their heads, leant forward and kissed them both. 'Wellmet,' she whispered. 'Art mushed?'

They nodded.

Mirl raised her head, spread her arms and demanded: 'Who among us claims Firstfall of Bitos, Son of Seedspiller?'

There were a lot of giggles and 'oohs' and 'ahs' from the darkness, then Mel heard his sister speak out clearly: 'I, Jo, daughter of Jud, claim Firstfall.'

Against a burst of clapping Mel turned and saw his sister step forward into the firelight. With her dark eyes fixed on the kneeling Bitos she slowly undid her belt, dropped it on the floor at her feet, and then slipped off her smock. It slid rustling to her ankles. Completely naked in the flamelight she raised her hands and made the lovely gestures of self-offering, touching first her eyes, then her lips and her breasts, and finally her thighs. Mel's heart melted within him but she had eyes only for Bitos who now bowed low before Mirl then rose to his feet and went through a mirror pattern of Jo's own gestures, offering her his Manhood, the flickering firelight gleaming on his strong young body. Mirl stepped forward, took Jo's left hand and Bitos' right and joined them. Then she took Jo's left hand and placed it on Bitos' ready yard. 'Take him,' she said, 'in Godsname.'

Amid a tremendous tumult of applause they moved off into the shadows.

Mirl turned back to Mel and winked at him. 'Who among us claims Firstfall of Mel, Son of Jud our Leader?'

There followed an awkward silence broken by a few whispers and a half-choked giggle. Mirl pulled a face and ran her red tongue round her lips. 'It looks as though I'll be taking it myself,' she grinned and called aloud: 'Again I ask who among us claims Firstfall of Mel, son of Jud our Leader?'

Softly from the shadows a voice called: 'I do.'

Mirl smiled at Mel who looked completely blank. 'Come forward and show yourself, whoever you are,' she commanded.

There was a scuffling in the shadows and out into the firelight stepped Frankie.

Mel's astonishment was so comical that Mirl burst out laughing, but the laughter died on her lips as Frankie unloosed her long silvergold hair, then her girdle and, giving Mel a little crooked smile, slipped her smock first from one shoulder then the other. Not for nothing had she vanned with the Actors. Instead of letting the garment fall at once as Jo had done, she held it for a moment to her breast and then, very slowly, released it.

Gravely, frowning slightly, she raised her slender arms, bent them and gently touched the four areas of offering one by one.

'Frankie?' Mel's whisper was an entreaty. 'Are you sure?'

Her frown faded. She smiled.

Mel turned slowly back and bowed to Mirl. She leant forward over him and whispered: 'Have you lost pride, boy?'

'Aye,' he muttered.

'No matter. You're not the first nor the last. Keep your back to the light.'

Mel rose slowly to his feet and turned to Frankie. He knew that he would never behold anything more beautiful if he lived till doomsday. In a slow dream he went through the formality of offering himself and at the joining of hands Mirl contrived to interpose her generous self between them and the watching Elds. As the applause roared out she drew them back with her into the shadows and whispered that not to be yard proud at such a moment was no shame. Then calling loudly for brew for all she launched Redeye into the Roamer Manhood hymn.

Frankie drew Mel down beside her into a nest of coverings. 'You see,' she murmured, 'I told you we should meet again.'

'But *how*, Frankie? How?'

'Jud came and found me. He's a very persuasive man your father. Not that *I* needed much persuading. He made some bargain with Fargal. I didn't ask what it was.'

'So *that's* where he went. The crafty old shugger! But how could I have guessed?'

'You looked as if you'd seen a ghost,' she grinned. 'I can't say I felt very flattered.'

Mel buried his face in her hair. 'Godhole,' he groaned softly. 'Oh *Godhole*, it's just a mush dream.'

'Don't you believe it,' she whispered. 'Look, I'm real.'

With these words she proceeded to show him what Manhood was all about and after Mel had died and been resurrected and died again she held him locked to her and whispered: 'So it *was* your first pluck. I'm glad.'

'You know?'

'I know.'

'Was it good for you too?'

She laughed softly. 'Fantastic.'

'You're just saying that.'

'No, it's true. I always wanted to take your firstspill. Ever since you put that chaplet on me in Fargal's van. Do you remember?'

'Remember! I dreamt about you for weeks.'

'Good dreams?'

'Not as good as this.' He drew his fingers lightly across her forehead and whispered: 'Does Father know you've been planted?'

'*I* haven't told him.'

'Did Fargal?'

'I don't suppose so. Why should he?'

'Why should he?' Mel repeated. 'Anyway it's too late for anyone to do anything about it now.'

She nodded and her fingertips strayed idly across his back. 'Jud told me how you'd been punished. He's very proud of you, you know.'

Mel snorted but was far from feeling displeased.

'Was it awful?'

'Yes,' he said simply.

'What had you done?'

'Jud didn't tell you?'

'He just said you'd been whipped.'

Mel disengaged himself from her and squatted back on his heels. Judging from the sounds around them the celebration seemed to be developing along the lines Old Negus had foretold. Someone came up behind Mel, flung her arms round him and he found himself engulfed in an enormous pair of naked breasts. 'Hey!' he protested. 'Shug off! Oh, it's you, Mirl.'

'Did he make it?' Mirl demanded, speaking to Frankie over the top of Mel's head.

Frankie laughed and produced the spillsac. 'Twice,' she said.

Mirl fingered the sheath judiciously. 'Ah, he's a good lad,' she said, patting her stepson's cheek affectionately. 'But he'll do better than that afore curfewsend. Bring us some more brew here!' She held Mel pinned back to her chest and said: 'Hey, boy, what was that trove offering you made?'

'Food,' he said.

'Who says so?'

'I do.'

'Well, none of us have ever seen its like.'

Someone came across to them, took the sheath of spill from Mirl and handed her a jug of brew. She drank deep then passed it to Mel. Frankie sat up. 'What trove offering?' she asked.

'His,' said Mirl, rocking Mel's head between her billowing breasts. 'Seems they were in two minds whether to take it. Where'd you glean it, boy?'

'Outside.'

Mirl laughed goodnaturedly. 'Spawn beds was it?'

'I told you. Outside.'

'And where's that?'

'One day I'll show you, Mirl. Soon maybe.'

'You're a good lad,' Mirl chuckled, 'but a bit of a dreamer. Lie still now and I'll show *you* a thing or two.'

Neither Mel nor Frankie were in any doubt that she could

have done so, but they pleaded with her and she relented. When she had gone Frankie said: 'Did you mean that about Outside?'

'Of course I did.'

'Is there such a place?'

'*Is there!*'

More or less chronologically he told her what he had been doing since their last meeting. She listened like one spellbound until he had finished then she said: 'It's like the last bud-in I had. That one I told you about. My first High.'

'How do you mean?'

'Well, just before I blew it I saw something like that. All those tiny specks of light in the blackness and a sort of round thing—but not silver like yours—sort of greeny blue. It was the loveliest thing I'd ever seen in my life and I suppose that's what made me do it. I just sort of reached out for it and pulled it towards me.'

'What happened?'

'Like I said. I blew it. Everyone in the circuit started screaming. But just before that happened—when I was still sort of reaching out—I seemed to hear someone calling *Who are you? Who are you?* Just like that. Wasn't that strange?'

'I don't think it *was* the same place,' said Mel. 'Arfaxis was *there*—I mean the Nightwatcher could *see* him.' he suddenly recalled one more inexplicable fragment from his hold of that memorable night. 'Arfaxis said he'd used *your* method. He somehow made the Nightwatcher agree to my cutting that trove and then he said he'd obtained permission "by Frankie's method". I didn't know what he meant.'

'You told him about *me*?'

'I didn't *tell* him. He must have read you in me—like I read Coney.'

Frankie suddenly gripped his arm with both hands. 'Take me Outside with you, Mel,' she implored. 'Soon. *Please.* Promise you will.'

'All right,' he grinned. 'It's a promise. We'll have to be careful though. I'm under Security watch.'

Frankie flung her arms round him, hugged him to her, and pulled him down on top of her. Mirl's short-term prophecy was fulfilled.

15

The Clan returned to the enclave next morning and, pending more permanent arrangements, Bitos and Frankie moved in to van with Mel and Jo. It was a happy time. Life was cramped but cosy. Dog was even allowed to remain in occupation of the spare cell. Frankie was introduced to the Partners and though she did not have the others' gift of reading a Partner's hold she straightway established a mysterious rapport with Dog. The true nature of the link was never established but its potential was made manifest a few days later when the four of them were down in the warrens and Frankie suddenly said: 'Dog's calling.'

Jo, who was standing beside her combing out a Partner, blinked. 'Who's calling?'

'Dog,' repeated Frankie, and then said: 'Mel, the Handlers are looking for you. They're talking to Redeye.'

Mel and Bitos came across and stared at her in disbelief. The warrens were twenty minutes' hard walking from the camp and they had left Dog shut up in the van. 'You mean you can—'

'Shh,' said Frankie. 'They're going over to Jud's van. Now

Mirl's come out. She's pointing along the Highway. The Handlers are walking back to their floater. Dog says they're coming here.'

'Are you *sure*, Frankie?'

She nodded emphatically. 'Dog says shall he come too?'

'You can *talk* to him? From *here*?'

'Yes.'

'Then tell him to stay where he is. If they get hold of him we'll never see him again.'

There was a moment's silence then Frankie said: 'He understands.'

Bitos guffawed. 'I don't believe it! No one can do that.'

Frankie flushed. 'You can read Partners,' she retorted. 'Lots of people would say no one can do that either.'

'That's different. They're *alive*. Dog's just a Factor—a machine.'

Frankie stamped her foot. 'He's not *just* a machine! He's Dog. Just as much as you're Bitos. And I'd trust him a lot more than some of these anyway!' She flung out a scornful hand towards the indifferent Partners.

Bitos shrugged cheerfully. 'Well, yes, I admit they're a pretty scruffy bunch. And as for that Coney I wouldn't trust him as far as I can spit. But it'll take a lot to make me believe you can talk to old Dog when he's more than a mile off down the Highways. How about you, Mel?'

But before Mel had time to say what he believed or why, they all heard the whine of an approaching floater. 'Well I'll be shugged!' exclaimed Bitos.

'What can they want, Mel?' asked Jo anxiously. 'You reported yesterday.'

Mel spread his hands and watched the floater come to rest ten yards from where they were standing. Two Handlers climbed out and walked towards them. 'Which of you two is Mel, son of Jud?' demanded one.

'I am,' said Mel.

'Can you read?'

Mel shook his head.

'Any of you others read?'

'I can,' said Frankie.

'Read that to him,' said one of the Handlers and thrust out a memory plate.

Frankie glanced at it. 'It's a Court Order,' she said.

'Just read what it says,' said the Handler.

'"By order of the powers invested in me by the Highest Authority I hereby deny to Roamer Mel, Son of Jud of the Jewellers' Clan, all access to Level 6 (known as the Deads) and all Intermediate Levels (known as the Fringes). Signed: Rol Makon Clerk of Court to Area Justice 17".'

The Handler took back the plate and turned to Mel. 'Put your print here, Roamer.'

Mel pressed the tip of his right index finger in the circular space at the bottom of the plate. 'But why?' he said.

The Handlers ignored the question. 'As from now, Roamer, if we catch you near the Deads or the Fringes we bring you in. Get it?'

'But . . .'

'No "buts". That's an order, communicated verbally in our presence and with your print on it. You break it: we break you.'

They turned away and walked back to their vehicle. Just as they were about to step inside one called back: 'And don't think this won't follow you, Roamer.'

'"Follow me"?'

'You lot are on Flit tomorrow.'

'*Flit!* Who says so?'

'Control.'

They were gone, leaving behind them only the cold sharp scent of ozone to tell of their passing.

'What's it all about?' demanded Bitos. 'Do you know, Mel?'

Mel shook his head. 'Why have they shut me out of the Deads? They could have done that when they sentenced me if they'd wanted to. And Father said we were staying here till after High. What's made them change their minds?'

'Let's get back to camp,' said Bitos. 'Maybe they'll know something.'

He was wrong. Apart from the stark fact that they must flit no one knew anything. The Clan accepted the order with that dour resignation to the inevitable that was habitual to them. After all, what was the point of asking questions when you knew no one would ever answer?

Mel sought out Jud and reminded him of what he'd said about staying on till after High. The Eld shrugged. 'They're not giving any reasons, son. I've just been up to Highway Control. We've got till noon tomorrow and that's our lot. You and Jo had better get started crating up the Partners.'

'Did you know they'd ordered me out of the Deads?'

'I heard.'

'Do you know why?'

'Don't you?'

'They wouldn't tell me. It was from Highest Authority though. The order said so.'

Jud sucked a tooth and eyed his son speculatively. 'Aye, that tallies,' he said.

'What do you mean?'

'I never did ask you how that lamp of yours came to be where it was. To my mind a boy's Challenge is his own affair. And I didn't ask how you came by that crazy trove offering. But my guess is someone up there's been putting two and two together and that denial order's what they've added it up to.'

'They *know* about my offering?'

Jud nodded.

'But *how*? Did you tell them?'

'They have their own ways of finding out.'

Mel stared at him. 'That voice . . .'

'I've lost you, son.'

'The one which accepted my Manhood. In the cave with the pictures on the wall.'

Jud spat. 'I want all those Partners crated and fooded by curfew. You make sure it's done.'

Mel watched his father walk away and then he turned and made his own way back thoughtfully to his van and passed on Jud's command to the others.

Three hours later the last of the Partners was securely fastened inside its crate and the crates were stacked ready to be loaded on to the trailer. Jo looked round at the warrens. 'I wonder how many of them will ever see this place again?' she mused.

Mel bent down, unfastened the catch on Coney's cage and lifted the Partner out by the scruff of his neck. 'You come with me, boy.'

'Where are you taking him, Mel?'

Mel winked. 'He wants his claws clipping.'

'Mel, he *doesn't*. I did it last week.'

'They've grown again.'

'Jud'll be furious when he finds out.'

'Why should he? Coney'll be back in time for loading.'

Jo's eyes widened. 'Oh, *Mel*!' she whispered. 'You're *not*! You're *crazy*!'

'Shut up,' he murmured. 'You know those shugging Eyes can read what you say. I'm taking him back with me to the van because his nails need clipping. All right?'

Jo bit her lips together and gave him a look which clearly said: 'I've got a raving idiot for a brother.'

In the security of the van he admitted blandly that he was going Outside. 'I promised Frankie,' he said, 'and it's the last chance we'll get.'

'What's this all about?' demanded Bitos. 'Where's "Outside"?'

Mel pointed upwards with his finger.

'The Deads?'

'Higher,' said Mel. 'As high as you can get. Where Coney tells.'

'Ah shug. That's crazy. We all know Coney's mushed.'

'Tell him, Jo.'

'It's there all right,' admitted Jo reluctantly.

'You've *seen* it?' Bitos was astounded. 'You never told *me*.'

Jo flushed and looked uncomfortable.

'How did you get there?' asked Bitos.

'Up one of the vents,' said Mel. 'Through the Deads.'

'Well, that's that then,' said Bitos with a chuckle. 'Those Handlers meant what they said, you know.'

'That's my risk not yours. And they won't catch me. Since when have they patrolled the Deads?'

'You mean you really *are* going?' Bitos' query was tinged with reluctant admiration. 'What's so special about this place anyway?'

'You've read Coney, haven't you?'

'Ah, don't give me that, Mel. You know Coney's mushed half the time.'

'Come with us then. See for yourself.'

'*No, Mel!*' Jo was aghast.

'Why not?' said Mel. 'There's no denial order on him. And we're not likely to have another chance. We may not be back here again for years.'

Bitos look at Mel, then at Jo, and finally back to Mel again. His eyes gleamed. 'All right,' he said. 'I'll go with you.'

Mel nodded. 'How about you, Jo? Have you forgotten "dream"?'

'You're mad,' she said. 'You really *are* mad, Mel. I thought once you'd got your Manhood you'd forget all that crazy Starson stuff. They'll kill you, you know that, don't you?'

'No one's going to kill anyone,' he said mildly. 'I just want to *see* it once more, that's all. All right then, so it'll be just the three of us. And we'll take Dog and Coney.'

'I didn't say I wouldn't come,' muttered Jo. 'I just said you were crazy.'

Mel grinned at her. 'Ah, you just want to keep your hands on Bitos.'

Jo's retort was merited, explosive, and most unladylike.

16

That evening there was a Clan gathering of the male Elds to discuss the Flit and it was an hour into curfew before Mel and Bitos returned to the van. Frankie and Jo were ready and waiting—Frankie bright-eyed and eager; Jo apprehensive and nervous. Mel rapidly outlined his plan which was that Jo and Bitos should start out first with Coney while Frankie and himself hung on for ten minutes and then followed with Dog. They were to rendezvous at the place they had nicknamed "Kobold's cave" and then make for the vent shaft. 'Once we're in the Deads we're safe,' he concluded and handed out the primed lamps.

'*We* may be,' remarked Jo sardonically and left the rest unsaid.

Mel scooped up Coney and passed him to her. 'Here's your first sucker,' he grinned. 'Looks just like his father.'

Jo smiled in spite of herself and slipped the Partner down the neck of her smock. Somehow she never found it easy to stay angry with her brother for long.

When they were alone Mel gave Frankie his spare knife and told her to belt it on. 'There's not one chance in ten you'll need to use it,' he assured her, 'but it might come in useful.'

Frankie unloosed her belt and threaded it through the slits in the sheath. 'You aren't frightened, are you,' she said and it was a statement rather than a question.

'No,' he admitted. 'The way I'm reading it, tonight's the one night they won't be expecting me to trespass. Not with that Order and the Flit tomorrow.'

'Would you still be going if I hadn't wanted to?'

'Probably not. It could be a night's good plucking wasted.'

She laughed. 'There'll be plenty more of those. This is different.'

The time candle sputtered.

'All ready, Dog?'

'Yes, Master.'

'Let's go then. You give us two minutes and then follow our trail.'

Mel snuffed the candle and slipped out into the enclave. There were lights still on in several of the vans and from under one of them came the clink of metal as Redeye made last-minute adjustments to a refractory floater. Frankie tiptoed to Mel's side. Like a pair of grey ghosts they flitted into the shadows and headed for the Deads.

Long familiarity with the route enabled Mel to steer clear of inquisitive Godeyes and twenty minutes later they crept into the Deads without having glimpsed a single patrol. They waited till Dog appeared and then let him lead them to the meeting place. 'Wellmet,' Bitos greeted them. 'Did you have any trouble?'

'Not a thing,' said Mel. 'And you?'

'Never known it so quiet.'

'Too quiet,' said Jo. 'I don't like it.'

Mel groaned. 'Godhole, Jo, anyone would think you *wanted* to trip a patrol.'

'I just said I don't like it,' she protested. 'That's all.'

'All right,' said Mel, 'just to make double safe we'll put out the lamps and hold on to each other's belt. Dog can keep us to the clearways.'

They arranged themselves in line and Dog held the end of a length of flex which Mel had brought as a lead for Coney. After a couple of false starts they got going and once they had grown accustomed to the new method they made surprisingly good speed. They stopped twice, once for Bitos to wet, and once because Jo thought she had seen a light. It proved to have been a false alarm. Finally Dog growled: 'We must turn off now, Master.'

'We'll light up again,' said Mel. 'No sense in breaking our necks. Two lamps will be enough.'

The light revealed the typical melancholy Deadscape, always half-familiar yet unknowable. Frankie shuddered. 'Is it all like this?'

Mel shrugged. 'Most of it, I think. Keep your eyes open for stray Strons.'

'What are they?'

'You'll know if you meet one,' he grinned. 'Come on. It's not far now.'

Five minutes later they reached the vent shaft. Mel put down the lamp he was carrying and gave the flex to Jo to leash Coney. 'Now for Godsake don't drop anything down the shaft,' he warned them, 'or I'll really be in the shug-hole. I'll go first, Frankie next, then Jo, then Bitos. Dog, you come last just in case someone slips. All right? Now someone shine the light over here.'

Bitos stepped forward, picked up the lamp Mel had put down and directed its light on the hatch. Mel gripped the wheel and twisted it. Nothing happened. He tried again. This time the rim moved a grudging inch. Swearing, he seized the two horizontal spokes, one in either hand, and—

'*Stay just where you are, Roamer!*'

A shaft of snow white light drilled out of the darkness and pinned Mel to the wheel.

'Don't move,' said a cold, flat voice. *'You are all under arrest.'*

A second beam sprang out and nailed the others. Jo moaned softly. The knot of terror within Mel slowly uncoiled. How many of them were there? 'They're not doing anything wrong!' he shouted. 'You can't arrest them!'

The reply was a blue flicker. The top left shoulder of Mel's tunic was a charred rag. *'Turn round, Roamer.'*

Mel slowly released the spokes of the wheel and turned, his eyes shuttered against the brilliance.

'Walk forward three paces.'

So there *were* only two of them. There was still a chance.

'Stand still.'

The second light was moving round as the other Handler came up behind him.

'Hands behind your back.'

He reached backwards slowly. The jaws of a metal cuff mumbled at one wrist and clicked home. *'Get him, Dog!'* he shrieked and flung himself sideways and back.

His shoulder crashed into the metallic chest of the second Handler. A ripple of hummingbird-blue flame streaked just over his head and a panel of the vent shaft glowed cherry red. He felt a steely talon fasten on his leg just below the knee and flailed out hysterically with the hanging cuff. By sheer chance it caught the lens of the Handler's lamp and shattered it just as the robot's other hand fastened on his throat. *'Dog!'* he screamed. *'Dog!'*

For one imbecilic instant he seemed to be looking downwards from the very roof of the Deads, then a jarring crash knocked the wind out of his lungs. The grip on his throat relaxed and he rolled clear. Something extraordinary was going on but he was too dazed to make out what it was. Why wasn't the other Handler firing? The remaining light beam was sweeping round and round like Mark's wheel of fortune, and in one brief flash of its passing he saw Jo crouched beside the vent shaft.

The Handler he had been grappling with lurched to its feet and groped towards him. Stumbling back, Mel snatched up the lantern and flung it. It smashed high up on the robot's chest. A yellow flameflower bloomed in the darkness. By the sudden blaze he saw Frankie standing beside Bitos, gazing at the other Handler which was staggering round in a drunken circle. Even as he watched, it crashed into a wall, teetered for a long moment on one leg and then measured its length in the dust, its limbs twitching spasmodically. The lamp it was still holding swept aimlessly back and forth cutting a swathe of light through the sooty shadow.

Frankie turned to the second robot. It took a hesitant step towards her, pawed stupidly at the flames round its neck, and then its knees buckled beneath it. 'Gwarp-gwarp,' it croaked in a puzzled fashion, 'gwarp-gwarp-gwar . . .'

Mel walked slowly back to it. Mustering all his strength he smashed the swinging metal cuff down at its blank sensors, striking again and again until each was splintered into an opaque mess. Then he moved across and did the same to the other.

'It's all right, Mel. It's quite dead.' Frankie's voice seemed to reach him from the end of a long long tunnel. A fearful puppet-like jerking plucked at his arms and legs. He sank down beside the wrecked machine and let his head droop between his knees.

'Are you all right, Mel?' (Bitos' voice.)

Mel drew a deep shuddering breath and raised his head. The effort the movement cost him was out of all proportion. 'What happened?'

'I'm not sure. Frankie did something to them. Are you all right?'

'Yes, I think so. Where's Dog?'

'Here, Master.'

'How long do you think we've got, Mel?' Bitos was kneeling beside him wrenching the lamp from the grip of the dead Handler.

'"How long?"' Mel echoed vaguely.

'Before they're on to us.'

Lethargy dropped from Mel like a shed skin. 'Perhaps an hour. Less probably.'

Frankie came up and handed him a black metal key. 'I think it opens that bracelet thing,' she said.

He took the key and began wrestling the cuff from his wrist. 'What did you do to them, Frankie?'

'I'm not sure,' she confessed. 'Anyway Dog got yours first.'

'I lifted him and dropped him,' said Dog with simple pride. 'He was very heavy.'

Mel managed a pale grin. 'You're a wonder, Dog. It was kind of you to drop him underneath.'

Dog growled. 'It just happened like that, Master.'

The other Roamers gathered around Mel. 'Whatever you did, Frankie, it worked,' he said. 'Almost too well.'

'What do you mean?'

'They'll hunt us down for sure. Not just me—all of us. We're outlaws.'

They stared at each other as the full import of his words sank in, then Frankie said: 'But why Jo and Bitos? They can't know about them?'

'They will,' said Mel grimly. 'Unless we can think of something, they'll have them inside Area Justice within an hour. By the time those Factors have finished with them they'll have told everything there is to tell.'

'But if they tell the truth . . .?'

'What "truth"? The truth is that two Handlers are dead and that four Roamers were concerned in it. They won't bother to divide up the blame. And when they discover *how* they died they'll make quite certain it never happens again.'

'He's right, Frankie,' said Bitos. 'We can't just hang around and wait to give ourselves up.'

'But where . . .?'

'Outside's the only chance,' said Mel. 'Where else *is* there? We'd starve in the Deads even if they didn't find us, and we wouldn't last five minutes in the Levels.'

'Come on,' said Bitos. 'We're wasting time. Let's try and get that hatch open.'

The four of them strained at the wheel but the mechanism had evidently been locked from the other side and after two exhausting minutes they were forced to give up. 'Isn't there some other way in?' gasped Bitos.

'I never saw one,' said Mel.

'How about that gun thing?' said Frankie. 'Couldn't you try that?'

They found the weapon lying where the Handler had dropped it. It was just a plain black tube about eighteen inches long with a button towards one end. Mel told everyone to stand well back, pointed it at the centre of the wheel and pressed the button with his thumb. Nothing happened. He tried twice more and then surrendered the tube to Bitos. For all the good they did they might as well have been pointing with their fingers.

'Let Dog try it,' said Jo suddenly.

'Are you serious?'

'Well, he's a sort of machine, isn't he? Maybe it only works for them.'

Mel shrugged. 'Go on then, Dog. What have we got to lose?'

Dog seized the tube in one of his grips, pointed it at the centre of the wheel and pushed the button. An ice-blue streak laced the intervening air. Within seconds the wheel sagged and clattered to the floor. Before it had come to rest the hatch swung outwards. Mel gave a crow of triumph and started forward.

'Wait, Master! It will be very hot. Let me go first. I will carry each of you up to where the tunnel bends.'

'He's right,' said Mel. 'Go on, Jo. You first, with Coney.'

'I haven't got Coney. He disappeared as soon as the fight started.'

'He'll have enough sense to look after himself. Off you go, Dog.'

Dog floated himself through the open hatch then, taking hold of Jo's wrists, drew her up into the tunnel after him. In two minutes he was back. 'You next, Bitos,' said Mel. 'I'll keep Frankie here in case another patrol shows up.'

'Do you think they'll follow us into the Outside?' asked Frankie.

'They may,' Mel admitted. 'I'm just guessing that they won't. The Nightwatcher didn't seem to know what I was talking about when I mentioned the Handlers.'

'Will they punish the Clan?'

'Why should they? That wouldn't find *us*.'

'As a warning to others maybe.'

Mel shrugged. The problem seemed so remote as to be almost unreal. 'Tell me what you did to those Handlers,' he said.

She frowned. 'I don't know how to explain. You remember the Random Arcade? Well, it was a bit like that. I sort of *thought* my way into them and—well, *altered* things. They're rather like Dog inside. I was just going into the one with the gun when you yelled for help. I think maybe, if I'd had a bit longer, I could have got them to open the hatch for us.'

Mel gaped. 'You *what*?'

She nodded very seriously. 'There was a sort of dark place in both of them,' she said. 'A sort of Deads. In Dog it's all light everywhere except for the shadowy bits he can't remember. I knew that if I could manage to get that place in them to light up they'd help us like Dog does, but when I tried to do it they just sort of died.'

Before Mel could question her further Dog had reappeared. 'You'd better go next,' said Frankie. 'I'll be able to look after myself all right.'

Mel handed her the light. 'You're just a human Coney,' he grinned and kissed her.

Three-quarters of the way through the ascent, Dog growled.

'What is it?' asked Mel.

'The engines are stopping, Master.'

'Is that bad?'

'I do not know, Master.'

'You leave me here, Dog. I can climb the rest. Go back and get your mistress.'

Mel felt his toes bump gently against the tunnel wall and then one of his wrists was released. He groped for the flange and found it. 'Right, boy,' he grunted. 'Off you go.'

Dog's whiskers brushed against his back in the darkness and that was all. He started clambering upwards and reached the bend in the shaft a few moments before Dog reappeared with Frankie.

'What happens now?' asked Bitos.

Mel squeezed past him. 'Follow me,' he panted and set off at a rapid crawl along the tunnel.

When he reached the side vent where he had hidden the ladder he offered up a silent prayer and plunged in his arm. His relief when he found the bundle lying exactly where he had left it was almost comical. At one breath his fears evaporated. He dragged the ladder out into the main vent and clambered with it up the final few yards into the base of the tower. As he did so he heard, far away in the distance, a series of dull thumps. 'What's that?' whispered Jo. 'Vent shields?'

Mel shrugged. 'Could be anything.'

'Listen!' hissed Bitos.

A faint, persistent, whining note, like a freighter starting up only higher-pitched, sighed out of the tunnel beneath them.

'Look!' cried Frankie. 'Above you!'

They all stared up. In the white beam from the Handler's light they saw two silvery sycamore leaves spiralling slowly down towards them. As they watched they all felt the cold breath of fresh air upon their upturned faces.

Mel was the first to realize what was happening. 'Come on!' he yelled 'Up to the top! Quick! Lift me. Dog!'

As he rose through a swarm of downward swirling leaves he shouted back to the others: 'Hang on! They're trying to suck us down! Dog'll come and get you!'

Fighting for his breath he clung to the grille with one hand and fumbled frantically to knot the ladder flex with the other while the inrushing wind tore at his hair and flayed the tears from his eyes. It was only after Dog had lifted Bitos to help him that he managed to get the first knot fastened.

As the force of the gale increased it sucked an eerie moaning from the grille, a sound which mounted steadily to a terrifying roar. Bitos clung to the bars on either side of the gap and buried his face in Mel's back. A branch of the sycamore, dragged backwards, crashed against the grille and howled as if in pain. A twig stripped of its leaves lashed savagely at Mel's cheek as he wrenched the second knot fast. Heaving up the bundled ladder he thrust it out with all his force. It bobbed for a moment as though undecided and then sank reluctantly out of sight.

Turning his back on it, Mel grabbed at Jo and lugged her to the grille. She opened her mouth and the wind tore inside her cheeks. He pummelled at her frenziedly until she somehow managed to force her way between the bars. As Frankie strove to follow her the howling wind snatched out her long hair and snarled it round the trapped branch. She clawed at it frantically, her eyes blind with terror. Mel grabbed the knife from her belt, slashed her free, and clambered after her. Bitos, the last to emerge, found himself crucified against the outside of the bars, nailed by the force of the hurricane, till Dog managed to prise him loose and lower him to the ground.

They lay slumped in the nettles where they had fallen and listened to the tower raging overhead. Then, as suddenly as it had started, the gale stopped. They heard the tortured branches of the sycamore creaking and groaning, and broken twigs, released from the grille, began to patter down in the darkness around them. 'Master,' Dog growled in Mel's ear. 'Master, we must go from here.'

Mel groaned and heaved himself up painfully until he was kneeling on all fours. 'The light,' he mumbled through bruised lips. 'Who's got the light?'

'I lost it,' muttered Frankie's voice from the shadows. 'I couldn't hold it.'

'Master, we must go. Hurry, Master.'

'Jo? Are you all right?'

Something grey stirred among the nettles beside him and Mel heard a stifled sob.

'Bitos?'

Above them the creaking of the tree died fitfully into silence.

'Ah shug,' came Bitos' resentful tones from the shadows. 'I'm being burnt alive.'

'We've got to move,' grunted Mel. Staggering to his feet he lurched across to Jo and pulled her up. 'Come on, Frankie,' he called. 'Quick!'

Like phantom toadstools their dim shapes rose up slowly from among the nettles and they limped painfully away down the slope from the base of the tower. As they reached the strip of rough grass that separated the tower from the edge of the cornfield Bitos gasped: 'Behind you! Look!'

They all turned and, as they did so, they saw that the grille had become subtly alive with a fragile lacework of crackling blue light. Twigs which had remained trapped between the bars burst into spurts of bright white flame. Before their awe-struck gaze the lacy azure trails seemed to drip downwards towards the base of the tower wrapping it round in rippling diaphanous folds. One after another the rungs of the ladder exploded in a series of sharp knucklebone cracks. The flickering web flowed on till it reached the ground. There it spread out till it was netting the area where, a moment earlier, they had been lying. Then it slowly crept inwards again, climbed back in fits and starts up to the summit and faded hesitantly away.

'Godhole,' muttered Bitos reverently. 'Those shuggers aren't joking, are they?'

Mel stared at the smouldering red pinpoints of fire that had once been his ladder and shivered. 'They must have wanted us alive,' he murmured. 'If they'd done that at first we wouldn't have had a chance.'

'What do we do now, Mel?' asked Jo.

It was a fair question but not one which Mel felt properly qualified to answer. It suddenly struck him that there was all the difference in the world between making a daring foray into the unknown secure in the knowledge that a snug van was waiting for you back in the enclave, and knowing that you were trapped on the Outside—a fugitive from the Law—the marked quarry of every Factor, every Plant, and possibly even every Roamer inhabiting the Levels. 'In Godsname,' he muttered, 'what have I done?'

'Dropped us right in the shug by the look of it,' grunted Bitos.

The justice of the observation was beyond dispute and Mel was in no mood to argue anyway. 'Well, we can't stop here,' he said. 'This is the first place they'll start looking for us.'

'All right then. Where?' demanded Bitos.

They all peered into the darkness about them but the night was almost as black as it had been when Mel and Jo had first ventured into the tower. There was no moon to be seen and, while Mel was still trying to decide which direction to take, the rain started.

When they felt the first chill drops splash down on them their instinctive reaction was blind panic. They dashed this way and that in a frantic effort to escape what they believed must be some diabolic device directed at them by their pursuers, and it took several minutes before they realized that its power was limited to making them wet and uncomfortable. By that time they were well and truly scattered. Had it not been for Dog who raced about like a desperate collie and rounded them up they might well have spent the rest of the night wandering blindly over the hillside. Jo, as it happened, had stumbled over one of the insulated rails and by the time Dog found her she was being interrogated by the pompous little Nightwatcher. Sprawled on the ground with tears and rain pouring down her cheeks and her hair plastered over her face like seaweed over a rock she obviously did not fit any of the robot's coded categories of identifiable human behaviour. It turned to Dog almost with a sigh of relief. 'It says it is a boo-hoo,' it complained. 'I do not understand. Is it yours?'

'Yes,' growled Dog.

'What is it doing?' demanded the Watcher.

'She is unhappy because she is lost,' said Dog. 'Come with me, Mistress.'

'Why do you call it "Mistress"?' enquired the Watcher. '"Mistress" and "Master" are terms to be addressed only to humans.'

'She *is* a human,' growled Dog, assisting Jo to her feet. 'You must help us to find shelter. It is your duty.'

'She has two bumps,' said the Watcher. 'Is she a woman? I have never seen a woman.'

'There are two women and two men,' said Dog. 'They are all lost. Where can we take them?'

'We can go to the Service Quarters,' said the Watcher. 'We have a man staying there.'

'How do we get there?'

'I will take her,' said the Watcher. 'Does she understand speech?'

'Of course she does,' said Dog. 'She is only wet and frightened. Mistress, will you wait here while I go and fetch the others?'

Jo gulped tearfully and managed to say 'Yes'.

Dog sped off into the darkness and the Watcher apologized for not having recognized her as a woman. 'I only met my first man a short time ago,' it informed her chattily. 'I must ask you to excuse me. Do women often go on four legs?'

'I fell over,' Jo gulped. 'Are you the Nightwatcher?'

'Yes, madam. Nightwatcher 278 stroke 394B3. At your service, madam.'

Jo gave a tremulous sniff. 'My brother told me about you.'

'Your brother is Mr. Arfaxis, madam?'

'Mel's my brother.'

'He is the friend of Mr. Arfaxis?'

'I don't know,' sighed Jo wearily. 'He didn't tell me about him.'

'It is a privilege to serve Mr. Arfaxis,' said the Watcher, then added blandly: 'It is a privilege to serve all humans.'

Jo sniffed lugubriously and, for no particular reason, began to cry again.

The Watcher observed this in some perplexity for a minute then said: 'Why does your face water, Madam? Do all women's faces water?'

Jo tried brushing her eyes with her forearm but the tears would not stop. All that happened was that her cheeks became smeared with mud.

'It is perhaps an effect of your bumps?' enquired the Watcher. 'Do they require lubrication? The Farmers and Harvesters all require frequent lubrication.'

Before she had a chance to enlighten it there was a shout from the darkness and Mel appeared with Frankie and Bitos. 'Dog says there's somewhere we can shelter,' said Mel. 'Is that the Nightwatcher?'

'Hello, sir,' said the Watcher brightly. 'The weather is rather inclement for strolling, is it not? I have been enjoying the privilege of conversing with your sister who is at present lubricating her bumps. Good evening, sir. Good evening, madam. I am Nightwatcher 278 stroke 394B3. At your service, ladies and gentlemen.'

'Can you carry the two girls?' demanded Mel.

'A pleasure, sir,' responded the Watcher and proceeded to demonstrate its willingness by lowering two sets of stirrups and raising a hoop.

'Sit on it, Frankie,' said Mel. 'It's quite safe. Jo, you hold on to her. How far is it, Watcher?'

'One thousand one hundred and seven metres, sir,' replied the Watcher promptly. 'Shall I transport these two ladies and then return for you gentlemen?'

'Yes,' said Mel. 'Go with them, Dog. Stay with them and make sure they're all right.'

'Very good, Master.'

As the incongruous quartet disappeared into the gloom, the rain began to fall with renewed vigour. 'I always said Coney was the worst shugging liar on four legs,' groaned Bitos and set off plodding disconsolately after them.

17

The Anthropologist had just finished transmitting his diurnal report when the Nightwatcher swished into the service bay with Dog trailing along behind like a small attendant zeppelin. He watched fascinated as first

Frankie, then Jo dismounted and gazed wonderingly about them. Rapidly reviewing the store of information he had absorbed from the Explorer he had already made a tentative identification before the Watcher sped back into the night. 'Jo?' he called experimentally. 'Frankie?'

The girls clutched at each other and peered fearfully about them. Dog glided towards him growling. The Anthropologist smiled. 'Allow me to introduce myself,' he said. 'My name is Arfaxis. I was wondering when we would meet.'

'Where are you?' demanded Frankie tremulously.

'He's here,' growled Dog, bristling his whiskers at the spot where the Anthropalogist was standing.

'Mel said there was a voice,' whispered Jo. 'I don't think it'll hurt us.'

'You look wet and cold,' said the Anthropologist. 'I suggest you would be wise to make use of the facilities provided. They don't appear to have been used for a very long time, but I assure you they are still perfectly serviceable.'

'Why can't we see you?' asked Frankie.

'That particular effect is one of the properties of the protective membrane I am enclosed in,' said the Anthropologist apologetically. 'I am hoping to be able to dispense with it before long but until your planet's ambience report is complete it is better not to take undue risks. I assure you I would much prefer to confront you as I am than as a disembodied voice.'

'You sound like one of the Clerking Factors,' said Jo suspiciously.

'That is because I have spent the last seven days acquiring my command of your language from the robots here. I can, if you wish, communicate with you non-verbally, but not with both of you at the same time. If you'll forgive me for asking what must appear a very stupid question—you *are* both Roamers are you not?'

'Yes.'

'Are there many of you?'

'Mel and Bitos will be here in a minute. The Watcher could only carry two of us at a time.'

'You misunderstand me. I was referring to your social unit—to all those like yourselves.'

Frankie shivered violently and the Anthropologist was immediately contrite. 'You really must come and have a shower and put on some dry clothes,' he said. 'There is a hostelry annexe with a Factor in permanent attendance. I was saying to it only this morning that it might be having some visitors soon. You can't imagine how delighted the little thing was.'

Jo and Frankie looked at each other doubtfully. Frankie said: 'I haven't had a shower for ten years.'

'What is it?' asked Jo.

'You stand there and warm water washes you all over and then you push a button and air dries you. It's fantastic.'

'I'd like some dry clothes,' said Jo. 'But what about Mel and Bitos?'

'Dog will tell them where we are,' said Frankie. 'Won't you, Dog?'

'Master said I was to stay with you,' said Dog.

'Dog will tell them where you are,' said the Anthropologist. 'Won't you, Dog?'

'Yes, Master,' said Dog simply.

'You did that, Arfaxis,' said Frankie accusingly. 'I saw you.'

The Anthropologist chuckled. 'Dog's a good dog, and you are a remarkably percipient young lady. Now if you will permit me to conduct you . . .'

The both felt an invisible hand alight in theirs and draw them gently forward towards a panel in the wall of the Service Area. As they approached it slid open and they passed through into a tiled corridor from which a dozen doors led off. 'Those are meditation quarters,' explained the Anthropologist. 'Really remarkably comfortable, I assure you. The showers are down here next to the feeding room.'

A door was thrust open ahead of them and the Anthropologist called: 'Hygiene Factor, here are the visitors I promised you!'

A shiny little robot popped out of a niche in the wall. 'Why, Mr. Arfaxis,' it chirped, 'how very kind of you. Step this way, ladies. Would you prefer lavender, verbena, or sandalwood?'

'Personally I recommend lavender,' said the Anthropologist. 'I found it a most fascinating olfactory experience. And now I had better go and receive your companions.'

The girls' hands were released and they both felt something solid brush past them. The door opened and closed again. They looked at each other, shrugged, and turned back to the robot. 'Lavender,' they said in unison.

The rainstorm apart, Jo had never in her life been wetted all over at once and she found the hot fragrant shower a bewitching experience. Once she had overcome her sense of assault, she surrendered herself to it as though to a lover. Dazed, pink and dreamy-eyed she emerged at last and stretched herself languorously on the towelled couch while a little mechanical Masseuse pattered all over her and stroked and coaxed away her bruises. That done she joined Frankie in the adjacent closet and together they surveyed the selection of garments the Hygiene Factor placed at their disposal.

The temperature in the Levels always remained constant within a matter of a few degrees and the everyday wardrobe of all Roamers was of the simplest utilitarian style. Faced with the sort of trousseaux that had graced women in the 22nd Century the girls found themselves in something of a dilemma. Experiments with brassieres and panties reduced them to helpless laughter and in the end they settled for what would today be called "pyjama suits" in a luminous synthetic material that hugged their slender forms by static attraction. On their feet they placed soft slippers and, with a final giggle at their images in the mirror, ventured out in search of their men.

They found them already in conversation with the invisible

Anthropologist who called out: 'Charming!' as they appeared and stood self-consciously awaiting the effect.

'Godhole!' exclaimed Bitos. 'What's that?'

Mel turned and his face broke into a grin. 'Are you two off to a Plant High or something?'

'Wait till you see what they've got for you,' said Frankie. 'Personally I rather like them.'

Bitos rubbed his eyes. 'I must be mushed. Those aren't *clothes*, are they?'

'Of course they are,' said Jo. 'And we've had a shower too. Go on, it's your turn now.'

Mel and Bitos looked at one another questioningly. 'All right,' said Mel, 'we might as well. Where do we go, Arfaxis?'

'Through the doorway behind the girls,' said the Anthropologist. 'They'll show you. And then I suggest we all assemble in the feeding room where we can continue our discussion in more convenient surroundings.'

They found the feeding room as much of a revelation as the shower had been. Only Frankie with her childhood experience of life in the Citadels had any point of contact with the dial-a-meal slots and even she—the only one among them who could read the menu—had no notion what the names implied. The one word any of them recognized was "choy"—the familiar beverage of the Plant food bars—and, since Arfaxis was not in a position to advise them, they all chose something different and agreed to sample each other's.

Arfaxis observed them with detached amusement as they speared morsels from one another's tray and chewed them quizzically. The food was basically the same staple nutrient that they were familiar with, but the automatic culinary magic which transformed it into "Midnight Eclair", "Rum Baba", "Venusian Chicken Supreme", "Vienna Schnitzel" and a dozen other mysterious dishes was completely new to them. They all overate grossly but, apart from a slight glassiness in their expressions, they did not appear unduly perturbed.

Jo and Frankie carried the empty trays back to the hatch and then the four of them sat round and looked at each other. On the point of saying something, Jo found herself snatched up in a tremendous yawn. Bitos caught it from her and then they were all at it. 'What are you doing?' asked the Anthropologist curiously.

'I'm sleepy,' said Jo.

'Me too,' groaned Frankie.

'What is "sleepy"?'

'Tired,' said Bitos, fighting a losing battle against yet another yawn. 'You know. Sleep. Lie down and close your eyes and wake up again.'

'Don't you do it then?' asked Mel.

'No,' said the Anthropologist. 'Do you do it frequently?'

'Every night if we can.'

'Isn't it what those other cells are for?' said Frankie.

'It's possible, I suppose,' admitted the Anthropologist. 'I naturally assumed they were meditation couches.'

'I don't care what you call them,' yawned Frankie, 'but I'm going to find one and use it. Coming, Jo?'

'I'll join you,' said Bitos. 'Sorry, 'Faxis, I'm shugged out. Mel'll tell you anything you want to know, won't you, Mel?'

Abandoned by his troops Mel felt as though all their concerted weariness had devolved upon himself. He rubbed his eyes and, making a supreme effort, said slowly: 'Arfaxis, will you wake us up if anything happens?'

'Such as what, Mel?'

'Handlers looking for us. Blue fire. Tha' sort of thing. Promise?'

'Certainly I will.'

Mel nodded. ''N' tell Dog . . .'

There was a long pause. His head sank forward on to the table.

'Tell Dog what?'

But Mel was fast asleep. The Anthropologist surveyed him quizzically for some minutes then, smiling faintly, he lifted him in his arms as easily as if he had been a baby and carried him gently into a vacant cell.

18

It was close to midday when Mel awoke. His first impression was that he was still in his van but, as he sat up in the cell and caught sight of his unfamiliar clothes, all the events of the previous night flooded back like some incredibly vivid nightmare. The only thing he could not recall was how he had come to be where he was. He lowered his feet to the floor, stood up, walked slowly across to the shughole and had a wet. Then he fiddled with a shiny lever till water bubbled up into a translucent bowl, splashed his face and wiped his eyes with his fingers. He was mildly astonished to find how calm he felt and, tracing this back, he realized that it derived from his instinctive trust in the mysterious Arfaxis.

He walked out into the corridor and, hearing voices from one of the other cells, went across to it. Bitos and Jo were wrestling affectionately on one of the couches and Frankie was lying back offering encouragement and advice from the other. 'Ah, Mel,' said a familiar voice. 'You slept soundly?'

'Arfaxis?'

'He's here,' said Frankie, pointing to a declivity at the foot of her couch. 'Go on, Bitos. Show him again.'

'I can't. I've just spilled,' panted Bitos. 'Now Mel's here you can show him yourself.'

'Show him what?' enquired Mel.

'How to pluck,' said Jo. 'He says he's never seen anything quite like it.'

'He hasn't even got a yard,' said Frankie. 'I felt.'

Mel grinned. 'And whose idea was this?'

'We were at it when he came in,' said Bitos. 'He thought we were fighting each other. I told him he should have been at the Manhood.'

'Do you do it at any time?' enquired Arfaxis. 'Or is there a particular season?'

'Whenever we both feel like it,' said Frankie. 'Come on, Mel. Let's show him. You'll have to move over, Arfaxis.'

The declivity vanished from Frankie's couch. She sat up cross-legged, peeled off her top garment and then reached out towards Mel.

'I wonder if you would permit me to contact one of you?' suggested the Anthropologist.

'Go ahead,' grinned Frankie. 'Which of us would you prefer?'

'Both? In sequence, of course. That is if you have no objections.'

'I don't mind,' said Mel and surrendered himself to pleasure.

Five minutes later, breathing rather more heavily, they asked him how he had found it.

'*Most* interesting. In fact I would almost go so far as to call it disturbing. A genuine physical manifestation of a psychic affinity. Potentially of enormous power. I really am extremely obliged to you both.'

'Drop in any time,' chuckled Frankie. 'Who knows, one day I may be able to let you share in having a baby.'

'That would be a tremendous privilege for me,' said Arfaxis. 'Genesis is the most exciting phenomenon in the cosmos.'

'How do *you* do it?' asked Mel.

'In your sense we do not,' said Arfaxis. 'We undergo periodic dissolution and reconstitution but we do not know birth and death as you do. Perhaps we are missing something.'

When they had all dressed again they went back to the feeding room and dialled another speculative selection. While they were eating they discussed their situation with Arfaxis, and it was during this conversation that it slowly dawned on them that he might not be a genuine native of the Outside. However, only Mel, and perhaps Frankie, were able to conceive of such a possibility. For Jo and Bitos their present whereabouts was simply another and different Level—a sort of Deeps which happened to be up instead of down. Above this there were presumably still other Levels stretching infinitely upwards—a concept which could have had very little meaning since for them, generally speaking, reality was structured horizontally. But Mel, remembering Coney's last tell of the silver bubble which had drifted down to the sand-spit, was able for a moment to spin a thread in his imagination which linked Arfaxis with what the little Partner had told. The thread dissolved again almost immediately but the concept remained and gave a new dimension to his recollection of his first encounter with the voice which had described itself variously as a "visitor" or a "stranger" or a "traveller".

Encouraged by the Anthropologist's probing questions they described their life in the Levels and the events which had driven them to their present predicament. 'And what do you intend to do now?' he asked curiously.

They looked at each other and no one could think of an answer. Finally Bitos said: 'If we try to get back the way we came they'll kill us for sure.'

'Who is "they"?' asked Arfaxis.

'The Handlers, of course.'

'But surely the Handlers only obey their orders?'

'Well, the Magisters then.'

'Is it the Magisters who have outlawed you?'

Bitos shrugged. 'Who else?'

'The Magisters take their orders too,' said Mel.

'Who from?' asked Arfaxis.

'It calls itself "Highest Authority". We call it the Godhole.'

'Is it a Plant?'

'I don't know. None of us have ever seen it. It's just a voice.'

'You've spoken with it?'

They all shook their heads and Mel said: 'You don't speak to *it*—it speaks to *you*.'

'Not to us,' said Jo. 'It doesn't speak to Roamers.'

'It did at the Manhood,' said Mel. 'I heard it.'

'Why do you call it the Godhole?' asked Arfaxis.

'It's always been called that,' said Bitos.

'Not by the Plants,' said Frankie. 'They call it "Holy Father". When we were little we were taught to sing:

Holy Father, Great and Wise;
Watch us with your Loving Eyes.
Keep us Pure and Free from Sin;
Feed us, Clothe us, Bud us in.'

'What does "Holy" mean?' asked Jo.

Frankie shrugged. 'The same as "Godhole", I suppose. It used to speak out of the holes. "Sin" meant being naughty.'

'What I can't understand,' said Mel, 'is why the Factors up here treat us the way they do. Down in the Levels they just ignore us. Except for Dog, of course. There must be a reason, mustn't there, Arfaxis?'

'Certainly there's a reason,' agreed the Anthropologist. 'Do we need to look further than the obvious? These have been designed to serve man. Those on the Levels have been designed to serve the purpose of "Higher Authority".'

'But there aren't any men here for them to serve,' protested Mel.

'Which, presumably, explains why there was no need to alter them,' remarked Arfaxis.

Frankie frowned. 'Then how do you explain Dog?'

'Dog I assume to be a survivor from some extinct species of Factor who has retained the pattern originally printed into him.'

'Do you mean that the Handlers were once like Dog?' Jo sounded incredulous.

'Their remote forebears must have been,' said Arfaxis. 'I daresay we might even find a reference to it in your Sagas if we knew what to look for.'

'But what *happened*?' demanded Jo.

'That I can only guess,' replied the Anthropologist. 'However, the likelihood is that at some point in the distant past men must have relinquished responsibility for their own welfare to a non-human intelligence—presumably one of their own creating. Perhaps there was some enormous catastrophe on a scale beyond any human powers of organization to deal with—your description of the area you call the "Deads" might well lend support to such a conjecture—and this super-intelligence was given authority to deal with it. At one stroke the servant became the master. The Factors were accordingly reprogrammed and the world as you know it came into existence.'

Mel gazed blankly at the empty space which the Anthropologist occupied. 'But you're saying God is just a Factor,' he whispered.

'I doubt if you would recognize it as such,' said Arfaxis. 'Nevertheless, in essence, I presume that must be so.'

Mel buried his face in his hands and tried desperately to come to terms with what Arfaxis had said. For the first time some of the bits of the jig-saw seemed to be fitting together but the pattern they made was so grotesque as to be all but unthinkable. 'But who *made* the Levels, Arfaxis?' he pleaded.

'Don't misunderstand me, Mel. All I am offering you is a

possible explanation. We have not yet arrived at a firm conclusion.'

'"*We*"?' said Frankie sharply. 'Who's "we"?'

'The er—research team,' said the Anthropologist vaguely.

'Where's that?' she persisted.

'Oh, we're scattered here and there.'

'Who *are* you, Arfaxis?'

'We think of ourselves primarily as observers, Frankie.'

'But where do you *come* from?'

'I'm afraid that wouldn't mean very much to you even if I were able to tell you.'

'Some other Level?' suggested Bitos.

'You *could* say that,' agreed Arfaxis carefully.

'Why are you here?' asked Jo.

It was a question to which the Anthropologist could give no simple and straightforward answer. He compromised. 'To assist you—if I can.'

'Do you think the Handlers will come after us?' asked the practical-minded Bitos.

'I should say that depends largely upon how dangerous you appear to "Higher Authority". The fact that they have not yet acted is not necessarily a good sign. My opinion, for what it is worth, is that they are still investigating the nature of the damage to the two robots. If they discover what I think they will, further measures are bound to be taken against you.'

'What *will* they discover?' asked Mel.

'That Frankie is potentially the most dangerous threat to their authority that has ever arisen in the Levels.'

Bitos gaped. '*Frankie?* Godstruth?'

'The fact that they had her and let her go suggests to me either that they were incapable of recognizing what she was,' said Arfaxis, 'or that her powers have developed phenomenally in the years since she was disbudded and became a Roamer.'

Frankie's blue eyes grew wide. 'What *am* I, Arfaxis?'

'A phenomenon, Frankie. In technical terminology a psychokinetic prodigy—possibly something more.'

'A *what?*'

'A psychokinetic prodigy,' repeated Arfaxis. 'What we call a "* * *"'—he emitted a low, musical whistle. 'What astonishes me is that you were able to keep it hidden for so long.'

'Keep *what* hidden?' cried Frankie.

'Your gift—your power to manipulate basic energy structures. Weren't you ever tempted to employ it on the Factors?'

Frankie shrugged. 'What Factors? Any powers I developed were fully occupied keeping yard high Actors out of my cell.'

'There was the Random Arcade,' said Mel.

'Oh, *that.* That was just fun.'

'You mean that the destruction of those Handlers was the first time you'd attempted to control a Factor?' said Arfaxis.

'Well, there was Dog, of course.'

'But apart from Dog?'

'Yes,' she said.

'Then you don't really know what you *can* do?'

Frankie shook her head. 'I can call Dog,' she offered shyly.

'You can *what?*' For the first time Arfaxis sounded almost startled.

'Oh, yes,' she smiled. 'That's easy.'

'From how far?'

'She did it from the warrens,' said Jo. 'That's over a mile.'

'*A mile!*'

'I don't think the distance matters very much,' said Frankie. 'I mean it didn't *seem* any different from when he was in the van and I was outside.'

There was a pause then Arfaxis said: 'Why exactly *did* they dis-bud you, Frankie? Did you ever discover?'

'Not really,' she admitted. 'I just blew the Gallery circuit somehow. They said I had, anyway.'

'What happened?'

Frankie shrugged and glanced across at Mel. 'I don't remember,' she said. 'It was a long time ago.'

'Ten years?'

'About.'

Mel was on the point of saying something when he felt Frankie's foot pressed hard against his leg. Her blue eyes regarded him guilelessly. 'Shall we go and have a look at Outside?' she said. 'After all, that's what you brought me here for, isn't it?'

'All right,' Mel agreed, somewhat mystified. 'Has it stopped watering?'

'Long ago,' said Arfaxis. 'And, incidentally, the word for that is "raining".'

19

Emerging from the equable artificial "daylight" of the hostel into the dazzling sunshine of an early September afternoon was an experience totally without parallel in their lives. Even Mel who had some inkling of what to expect from his readings of Coney was half stunned by the sheer magnitude and brilliance of the scene. The others were overwhelmed and shattered. They simply could not come to terms with the perspective. They saw the clouds and the shadows of the clouds and thought they were no bigger than a handkerchief. Nearby butterflies and far-off seagulls were virtually indistinguishable. Only the towers, striding away for ever into the blue distance, seemed to drag their senses reeling after them. Instinctively they reached out and grasped at one another for reassurance. The sensation Mel had once experienced on his own now submerged the others. They felt diminished to pygmy size, lost. And then, as he had done, they passed through it and emerged upon the other side. They looked at each other, at the ground upon which they stood, at the silver thread of the Watchers' rail wandering away down the hillside, and a strange new realization dawned within them. The strained lines round their lips and eyes faded slowly; they drew in deep breaths of the richly scented air, and they smiled. Mel raised his arm and pointed down the slope to where the waters of the estuary twinkled in the sunlight. 'Come on!' he cried. 'It's all ours!'

The Anthropologist stood and watched until they passed out of his sight, and he experienced a twinge of an emotion which closely resembled old-fashioned human envy though he had no means of recognizing it as such. Of all the multifarious life-forms he had encountered throughout the galaxy, these children alone seemed to have the power to reach down into him and touch something so fundamental that hitherto he had barely acknowledged its existence. For a moment he permitted himself the luxury of remembering his own home and then, with a faint shrug, dismissed the thought. On the point of turning his attention to the technical problems connected with the transmission of the information he had just acquired, he heard the great sliding doors that closed off the Farmers' quarters purring open. Glancing round he saw a huge silver Harvester edge forward to the ramp, tilt itself ponderously and then coast down towards him. Knowing that he was clearly visible to its sensors he strolled out of its path only to see it check hesitantly in its progress, swivel, and then head straight for him. He reached out into its circuits to immobilize it and—nothing happened! Reflexes dictated. He jumped. The silver monster hurtled past, missing him by an armslength. He doubled back and crouched in the shelter of the ramp just as the second leviathan appeared at the top and began its descent. As it passed he probed tentatively into its simple brain, encountered the interference shield he now expected, and kept well out of reach.

The first machine, having lost track of him, turned back on to its original course and moved off down the hill, followed by its companion. As he stared after them he saw, far off, the sun glitter on a third machine and, beyond that, a fourth. Was it just coincidence? He scrambled under the ramp and hurried to the vault which housed the Watchers. As he approached, one of them emerged and fled shrieking down the rail and out of sight. Instinct made him pause. He took a hesitant step forward and called softly into the darkness.

As the sound left him, a frail reticulation of violet light flickered like an eyelid deep within the shadowy recess, and a single feathery filament rippled out hungrily along the rail towards him. It told him all—and more—than he wanted to know! Turning on his heel he ran back towards the hostelry. 'Dog!' he called. 'Dog! Dog!'

He found the little Factor lying in a corner. It did not stir at his approach. He probed cautiously and, at the instant of contact, prudently withdrew his mind. Even so the shock he received made him stagger. His respect for his antagonist increased a hundredfold and with it his fears for the safety of the young Roamers. He hurried outside and scanned the hill-side. The Harvesters were now spread out in a long glittering line which stretched in a vast semi-circle around the bight in the estuary. He counted no fewer than ten and, even as he watched, the one at the far end of the line reached the margin of the bay, turned slowly inwards, and began forging ponderously along the top of the low cliff, its silver flails flashing in the sunshine. At the same instant he saw two tiny, poppy-bright flickers, as first one and then the other girl darted out towards the headland, seemingly oblivious of their danger.

The Anthropologist started running down the hillside but had taken no more than a dozen steps before he realized it was hopeless. He saw the two little scarlet figures of the girls joined at the cliff's edge by the blue and white of the two boys, and he imagined them gazing out breathlessly across the estuary, pointing out their discoveries to each other, ignorant of the threat at their backs. Restricted by his protective membrane he guessed that any attempt to reach them telepathically at such a range was foredoomed to failure. Nevertheless he made two unsuccessful attempts. Then, on the point of surrendering to the inevitable, he found his fingers were fumbling for the seal which ran diagonally across his body from hip to neck. His action was totally irrational, possibly suicidal, and, within his ordained code, probably criminal, yet he did not hesitate. For one instant he appeared to be clothed from head to foot in a milk-white mist, then—

—*'Arfaxis?'*

—*'Frankie, you are in great danger. The Factors are hunting for you. Get down into the place where the stream flows. Hurry!'*

—*'Where are you, Arfaxis?'*

—*'At the Service Quarters.'*

—*'Are you all right?'*

—*'Yes, yes. Hurry now! And keep away from the rails.'*

The Anthropologist's lungs heaved with unaccustomed effort. His twin hearts pounded, established a new rhythm and settled into phase. His vision cleared and became crystal sharp. He saw the pygmy figures turn, consult for a moment and then scamper away towards the gulley. He drew a deep, experimental breath, exhaled it slowly, and then having peeled himself free from the now useless membrane he emerged into total visibility and set off down the hillside.

One of the Harvesters sighted the four Roamers just as they reached the lip of the gulley and, with one accord, the whole line paused then swung in towards them. Bitos glanced back, missed his footing and tumbled headlong down the grassy slope into a bramble thicket. The others slithered down to him, pulled him free, and then, skidding and scrabbling for a foothold, glissaded to the bottom. They wriggled their way under some bushes and peered out fearfully. A minute later the first of their pursuers clattered up over the skyline, forged forwards to the lip of the incline and then stood, teetering precariously over the precipitous slope, the silver blades of its flails whirling impotently. As they watched, a second monster lumbered up to join the first and went through precisely the same indecisive manoeuvres.

'What are we going to do?' whispered Jo.

'Maybe they'll go away if they can't see us,' said Mel. 'Did Arfaxis say why they were after us, Frankie?'

'He just said they were hunting us.'

'Here comes another,' muttered Bitos as a third juggernaut appeared on the opposite lip of the gulley. 'Just look at those shugging knives! Talk about instant processing.'

'I'm going to try and reach one of them,' said Frankie suddenly.

'Don't,' said Jo. 'They'll know we're here for certain if you do.'

'They know anyway,' grunted Mel. 'Just look at them. Go on then, Frankie. Give it a try.'

Frankie wriggled forward until she could clearly see one of the machines, then she pushed the hair up out of her eyes and stared upwards. The Roamers held their breath and glanced back and forth between her and the Harvester. A few seconds later she laughed excitedly. 'I've done it! Watch!'

As she spoke the whirling flails slowed jerkily to a halt and then the machine began edging back from the brink of the gulley. With her blue eyes sparkling Frankie turned her attention to the second.

In rather less than five minutes all the machines which had reached the gulley had backed away and were standing as placid as grazing cows. Frankie scrambled to her feet, skipped across the stream and began clambering up the slope towards them. 'Come on!' she called. 'They're quite safe!'

Somewhat less confidently the others emerged from their hiding place, then having observed Frankie deal casually with a late-comer, they recovered their courage and hastened to join her. They gained the top of the slope just in time to see the Anthropologist jog-trotting towards them.

Frankie waved cheerfully to him and gestured round proudly at the docile purring monsters which dwarfed her. 'Hey, what have *you* done to yourself?' she demanded.

'What have *you* done?' he countered. 'The two I tried to reach had an opacity screen of more than 4***!'

'Oh, was that what it was?' said Frankie. 'Well, they're all right now.'

'*You mean you broke it?*'

Frankie shrugged. 'I don't know. It was a bit harder than the Handlers, I suppose, but not much. They're *big*, aren't they?' She turned from satisfied contemplation of her handiwork back to the Anthropologist. 'Why, you look just like us,' she laughed. 'I thought at least you'd have green hair and red eyes.'

The Anthropologist regarded her with something very akin to awe. 'Don't you *realize* what you've just done, Frankie?'

She rubbed her nose with the back of her hand and grinned. 'You should have seen us getting down that slope, Arfaxis. Bitos went like a floater. I think he only touched ground twice.'

The Anthropologist eyed her narrowly but she carefully avoided his gaze and when he attempted to read her he found she had sealed off access to her own mind with an opacity shield of considerably more than 4*** . His inherent sense of superiority underwent a severe mauling. It took another w[illegible]e[illegible] the last of the outlying Harvesters appeared over the far horizon more than a mile away. Frankie caught sight of it, frowned for a few seconds, and then grinned. As she did so the machine stopped, turned in its tracks and lumbered back the way it had come.

'Hey!' cried Bitos admiringly. 'Did you see that, Arfaxis?'

Frankie laughed then wandered across to the nearest Harvester and climbed up on it. She peered around curiously for a moment or two and then clambered down again. 'What shall we do with them?' she asked. 'Send them back where they came from?'

'But if we do, won't they simply send them after us again?' said Jo.

'I thought maybe I'd sort of screen them off first,' said Frankie, almost apologetically. 'Like I did with the last one.'

'You did *what*?' cried Arfaxis.

'Sort of screened it off,' said Frankie. 'Like this.' She looked up at the behemoth from which she had just descended and then waved her hand vaguely towards the Anthropologist. 'Now try,' she offered.

Arfaxis looked from her to the machine and then shrugged. 'You've simply destroyed it.'

'I *haven't*!' Frankie sounded genuinely affronted. 'Look!'

The Harvester purred into life, trundled backwards for about twenty yards, then turned and set off in the direction from which it had come.

The Anthropologist gaped after it. 'But that's not possible,' he said faintly.

Mel laughed. 'She's getting better at it all the time, isn't she? Go on, Frankie, try something else. Call up old Dog.'

'Wait! Dog's been tampered wi—'

Before the Anthropologist could finish his sentence Frankie gave a sudden gasp of pain, clapped her hands to her head and sank down till she was kneeling on the grass at their feet. Arfaxis leapt to her side, pulled back her head, brushed aside her hands and gazed into her eyes. The lines of pain faded slowly from her forehead and she smiled palely up at him.

'Serves me right for being so yardy,' she whispered. 'Dog's all right though. He's coming.'

Arfaxis stared down at her in total disbelief. What she was claiming to have done would have tested the concerted powers of half the research team. That she had emerged from the contact alive was in itself a miracle: one could excuse the attendant aberration, but that is what it was.

Mel and Jo crouched on either side of her and gazed at her anxiously. 'What happened, Frankie?'

She blinked, shook her head as if to clear it, and pressed her fingertips to her temples. 'I don't know,' she confessed.

'Do *you* know, Arfaxis?' asked Mel.

'Whatever it was that sent the Harvesters out after you, got hold of Dog,' said the Anthropologist. 'I discovered it just before I warned you they were hunting you. He'd been suppressed and fed a lethal psychic charge. I still don't know what saved you, Frankie. Possibly the distance combined with your own opacity scre—'

'Hey, look who's here!' cried Bitos.

Frankie struggled to her feet and then, without warning, burst into tears.

'You called, Mistress?'

Everyone except Frankie drew back from the little robot which was hovering in the shadow of one of the Harvesters.

Arfaxis contemplated it incredulously for a long moment then announced: 'It's all right. He's completely discharged.'

'Of course he's all right,' gulped Frankie. 'I said he was, didn't I?'

'But how—?' began the Anthropologist. He swung round to Frankie, opened his mouth as if to say something and then, presumably unable to find the words he wanted, closed it again.

'What happened, Dog?' said Mel.

'"Happened", Master?'

'Did you go into the Watchers' quarters?' demanded Arfaxis.

'Yes, sir, I did,' growled Dog. 'They asked me in. Was I wrong to do that?'

'Of course not. We just want to find out what happened there.'

'I talked with the Watchers, sir. They are very excited that humans have come back to live with them. They are very friendly, sir.'

'And that's all that happened?' asked Mel.

'Yes, Master. I think so.'

'You don't sound very sure.'

'I cannot recall leaving their quarters, Master,' said Dog unhappily. 'But when the Mistress called to me I was outside. Did something bad happen?'

'Yes,' said Mel. 'We don't know what though.'

The Anthropologist turned back to Frankie. 'The instant you reached Dog. Can you remember what happened?'

Frankie drew a deep breath and let it out in a series of slow gasps. 'There was a sort of bright light,' she said hesitantly, 'and then everything went very small and far away as though I was somewhere miles up there'—she pointed skywards—'and I sort of heard myself calling to Dog, telling him to come here. Then I was back in me again and my head was aching.' She shrugged and wiped her cheeks with her sleeve. 'It was really quite a nice feeling except for the end part,' she said. 'A bit like being budded in.'

Arfaxis nodded. 'Do you feel any different now?'

'Not really,' she admitted. 'It's hard to say. Why?'

'Do you mind if I try a little experiment with you?'

She eyed him warily. 'What do you mean?'

'I just want to read you—to try to find out what's been going on. Will you let me?'

'Are you sure you know what you're doing?'

He nodded. 'Yes, I think I do, Frankie.'

'And what if you think wrong?'

'There is certainly an element of risk,' he admitted. 'I will be very careful.'

'All right,' she agreed reluctantly. 'What do you want me to do?'

'Just lower your screen a fraction.'

She glanced at him and, for an instant, the pupils of her eyes seemed to become enormous. The effect on the Anthropologist was dramatic. He reeled, tripped over his own feet, and sprawled his length on the trampled grass.

'Godhole!' gasped Mel. 'What have you done to him?'

'He's all right,' said Frankie. 'You are, aren't you, Arfaxis?'

The Anthropologist heaved himself up into a sitting position and muttered something unintelligible in his own language. Mel went across to him and patted his shoulder. 'You aren't hurt, are you?'

'His nose is bleeding,' observed Jo.

'Well, did it work, Arfaxis?' asked Bitos. 'Did you find anything out?'

The Anthropologist tilted back his head and sniffed plaintively. 'Oh yes, it worked,' he admitted ruefully. 'Almost too well.'

Frankie eyed him regretfully. 'I *did* warn you, didn't I?'

He nodded. 'I have only myself to blame, though I could hardly have expected anything like that.'

'Just what *is* going on?' demanded Mel. 'Do *you* know, Frankie?'

'No,' she confessed. 'It's something to do with what happened when I called Dog, isn't it, Arfaxis?'

He nodded. 'That psychic charge Dog was holding had to go somewhere. It was designed to annihilate whoever had the ability to contact him. If I had done what Frankie did I should now be dead. Yet she has simply absorbed that charge. I confess I cannot begin to understand *how* she has done it, but I am quite certain that is *what* she has done.'

'I *felt* something had happened,' said Frankie apologetically. 'I just wasn't sure what it was. I'm sorry, Arfaxis.'

'You still *look* the same,' said Jo surveying her minutely. 'Will it make any difference to her, Arfaxis?'

The Anthropologist made use of Mel as an aid to regaining his own feet. 'Unquestionably, it will,' he said. 'And I suspect that she is already at least as aware of the difference as I am.'

For the first time since the incident Frankie laughed. 'Why do you call yourself "Arfaxis"? Your name is ***. And you've forgotten that *** warned you that you might find something sophisticated.'

The Roamers stared at her in blank astonishment. As far as they were concerned she was talking pure gibberish. The Anthropologist smiled wryly. 'So much for my little experiment,' he said.

Mel was the first to grasp what had happened. 'She's *read* you!'

Arfaxis nodded. 'It would appear so. No doubt I deserved it. However, the consequences may well prove extremely awkward.'

Frankie looked down at her hands and then stroked them slowly all the way down her body to her knees. Her eyes sparkled with mischief. 'Don't worry, ***,' she chuckled. 'We'll look after you.'

'Thank you,' replied the Anthropologist gravely. 'I hope that will not prove necessary.'

Frankie clapped her hands and then hugged herself. Her face was like a pool of clear water brushed this way and that by the fickle breezes of a dozen different emotions. 'I . . .' she gasped, 'I . . .' and then broke off into peals of laughter.

The others regarded her with mingled apprehension and dismay. 'Are you sure you're all right, Frankie?' Mel asked.

'More than all right!' she cried. 'Much, much more. Oh *Mel* . . .!' But what she wanted to tell him was altogether beyond her powers of expression.

The Anthropologist said something to her that none of the others could understand and she replied in his own tongue as though to do so were the most natural thing in the world. Then she flung her arms round Mel and kissed him wildly. 'I'm sorry,' she gasped. 'I've just grown up, that's all. All of a sudden.'

He shook his head and grinned at her. 'You're crazy, Frankie. Really you are.'

'Crazy?' Again she kissed him a slow open-mouth kiss that made his toes curl and then drawing back from him said simply: 'Oh, Mel, I've never felt happier in my whole life! Never! *Ever!*'

He laughed. 'You really are a bit mad, you know. But who cares? I don't.'

She smiled at him and was about to say something when suddenly she held up a finger, appeared to listen intently, then announced: 'Coney's here somewhere.'

'Coney? Don't tell me you can read him too!'

'He is,' she affirmed. 'Go on, call him.'

Mel grinned. 'If you say so.' He put his hands to his mouth and gave the peculiar whickering call they used to summon the Partners. Nothing happened. Frankie just shrugged and repeated her assertion.

Bitos said: 'Is it safe for us to go back to the hostel?'

They all looked at Arfaxis who simply shrugged and passed the question across to Frankie.

'How can *she* know?' said Jo.

The faint hint of resentment in her friend's tone did not escape Frankie. She flushed and looked down at the ground and shook her head.

Arfaxis smiled and murmured something in his own tongue which, roughly translated, meant 'omniscience brings its own problems.'

Frankie looked up, seemed about to retort and then grinned. 'That Harvester I sent back is causing some problems too. I think we ought to send the rest back as well.'

'Then do it,' said the Anthropologist. 'You don't need my help.'

Without even bothering to look round Frankie set the great machines in motion and despatched them back to their quarters. As he watched them go Bitos observed: 'We might have thumbed ourselves a lift if we'd thought of it.'

'*Is* it safe for us to go back, Frankie?' asked Jo.

Frankie caught the Anthropologist's eye and smiled. 'I'm not sure, Jo,' she said. 'There's something going on all right, but I can't be certain what it is. They're still trying to make out what I did to that first Harvester I sent back.'

'Well, what *did* you do?' demanded Bitos.

She grinned. 'More or less what they did to Dog, but not in quite the same way. I just wanted to warn them to leave us alone. The trouble is I can't be sure if they've got the message. I think it will be safer if we wait till the rest of them get back.' She turned to Mel. 'Shall we go down and have a look at the water?'

'Why not?' he agreed. 'After all, it's what you came Outside for, remember?'

20

They descended the gulley in single file accompanied by Arfaxis and Dog. Halfway down Jo called excitedly: 'Look! There's Coney! You were right, Frankie!'

'How *did* you know?' asked Mel.

'I sort of heard him,' said Frankie vaguely. 'I didn't know where he was, though. Is he all right?'

Jo had scrambled up to where the little animal was crouched. 'His coat's in a terrible mess,' she said, lifting the Partner by the scruff of his neck and burying her face in his fur. 'Where have you been, boy?'

The others waited expectantly but a minute later she raised her eyes and shook her head in perplexity. 'It's all mixed up,' she said. 'And it's so dark I can hardly recognize any of the places. You have a go, Mel.'

'Let's wait till we get down,' said Mel. 'Here, I'll carry him.' He reached up to Jo, took Coney from her and set off down the bed of the stream.

A few minutes later they emerged on the beach and gazed mystified at the little channel the rivulet was busily scoring out for itself across the damp sand. Frankie removed her slippers and paddled her bare feet in the water. A swirl of sea-gulls, nonplussed by these extraordinary intruders, gyrated round them shrieking abuse, while high overhead puffy white clouds trailed shadows across the sandbars and patched the emerald water with splashes of purple. The very air seemed to vibrate with the shimmer and glitter of a life so strange to them it seemed totally magical. As the potency of the spell overcame them first Frankie, then Bitos and Jo started to run and jump, flinging themselves into the air, shouting and laughing and kicking rainbow showers out of the pools. Mel watched them until he too could restrain himself no longer. Thrusting Coney into the Anthropologist's arms he kicked off his moccasins and raced across the sand to join the others.

At last, breathless, flushed and bright-eyed they trooped back up the beach and flung themselves down on a sun-warmed dune. Bitos displayed the handful of shells and pebbles he had gleaned. 'There's a fortune here waiting to be picked up,' he announced. 'Just think what old Seedspiller could do with that lot! Look at those colours!'

The mention of the Clan reminded Mel that Coney was still unread. He reached out and took him back from Arfaxis. Settling the Partner down in the sand beside him, he lay back and closed his eyes. 'Tell, boy,' he commanded.

Coney wriggled joyfully and thrust his muzzle up against Mel's temple.

Long inured to the routine of Partnership the three Roamers paid scant attention, but the Anthropologist was fascinated. 'Can *you* do that, Frankie?' he whispered.

She shook her head. 'Partners aren't like Dog. With them it's just pictures.'

'But you've read me.'

'Maybe I could read one now,' she said indifferently. 'Godstruth, Arfaxis, I still don't know what I *can't* do!' She scooped up a handful of the fine white sand and let it trickle slowly through her fingers. When it had all poured away she said: 'Watch this.'

A thin plume of twinkling silica grains began to waver *upwards out of the dune*, growing up into her cupped palm like a tiny inverted tree, until her hand was filled to overflowing. She emptied it out and brushed her hand across her thigh. 'You see?' she said.

'So *that's* what you were laughing about,' murmured the Anthropologist. 'Do you know *how* you are doing it?'

'No,' she said and then added with a frown: 'I think maybe I will when I've found out *what* I am.'

She picked up a pinch of sand, placed it in the centre of her palm and peered down at it. 'It's just a lot of little tiny Dogs,' she grinned and puffed it over him.

Mel sat up and rubbed his eyes. 'You're right, Jo,' he said. 'It *is* all dark. Even the Highways. What do you think's going on?'

'Did you find the Clan?' asked Bitos.

'No. The vans have gone, and there's no sign of any Partners in the warrens.'

'You don't suppose they've arrested everyone?' said Bitos.

'All I know is what he tells,' replied Mel. 'Have a look for yourself.'

'Coney always tells me lies,' grunted Bitos. 'But I've never heard of the Highways being dark after curfewsend. Have you?'

'No,' said Mel. 'But they are.'

'Is it something to do with us?'

'Godhole, Bitos, how do you expect *me* to know? Anyway there's nothing *we* can do about it. You aren't telling me you're ready to risk that tower again, are you?'

'Shug, *no*!' Bitos shivered. 'Have *you* got any ideas, Arfaxis?'

The Anthropologist brushed some sand grains from his chin. 'I think it's probable the darkness *is* connected with your escape,' he said. 'Assuming they have had to draw on emergency power supplies from this area, the Levels in the immediate vicinity would be the first to feel the effect.'

'But what about the Clan?' asked Jo. 'Are they all right?'

'For the time being, probably, yes,' said the Anthropologist. 'What happens to *them* will very much depend on how badly your enemies want *you*. If they decide it's safe to ignore you then they gain nothing by retaining your friends as hostages. If, on the other hand, they *cannot* ignore you . . .' He spread his hands eloquently.

'But how will we know?' asked Bitos.

'They will inform us, I'm sure,' the Anthropologist assured him and smiled faintly. 'Our main problem is whether they will prove amenable to reason.'

'Do you think they will?' asked Mel.

'Madness has its own logic,' replied the Anthropologist. 'The true madman *knows* he is sane. That is his strength. Since for the rest of us sanity is largely consensus of opinion, he has an enormous advantage. Do you follow me?'

'I don't follow a shugging word,' said Bitos. 'Who's *mad*?'

'That's one of the things we have yet to discover,' said the Anthropologist. 'In their view *we* are.'

'*You* are,' said Bitos and looked as if he meant it.

'Precisely,' nodded the Anthropologist, apparently not in the least put out by the suggestion. 'You see, Bitos, from their point of view we—I take the liberty of including myself among you for the purposes of my argument—we, by violating the Law, have proved conclusively that *we are insane.* To assume, as we are doing, that to escape from the Levels was the action of sane people, is in fact no proof of sanity. On the contrary, in their view, it—'

'It is to *me*,' Mel broke in.

'But only because you had the temerity to question the Law,' said the Anthropologist.

Mel looked round at the glittering, sunbright estuary and shook his head. 'To want to see this was *mad?*' he protested. 'It doesn't make sense.'

'But who, apart from ourselves, even knows that this exists?' asked Arfaxis.

'Well, they do, of course.'

'"They" being whom?'

'Whoever it is who's been trying to kill us.'

'And who's that?'

'Higher Authority.'

'Which is . . .?'

'Well, God, I suppose,' he muttered.

'And what is God?' pursued Arfaxis relentlessly.

'"God is the Law",' said Jo, chiming in automatically with the final response of her childhood Catechism.

'A pretty circle,' commented the Anthropologist, 'but it does not get one very far.'

Frankie who had been lying silently listening to the conversation now said: 'Perhaps we can change the Law.'

Bitos grunted. 'You can't change the Law. The Law's the Law. It just *is*.'

'Because a thing *is* doesn't mean you can't change it,' she said. 'What's that white thing up there called, Arfaxis?'

The Anthropologist followed the line of her pointing finger. 'It's called a "cloud" in your language,' he said. 'We call them "***".'

'Watch it, Bitos,' she said.

The little cloud faded, faded, and was no longer there.

Even the phlegmatic Bitos was impressed. 'Godhole! Did *you* do that, Frankie?'

She nodded. 'You see, you *can* change things. You just have to want to do it badly enough.'

'I fear your God may prove more intractable than water vapour, Frankie,' murmured Arfaxis.

'There are some things even you can't know,' she retorted.

'Certainly there are,' he agreed. 'But you must not make the mistake of underestimating your opponent. I assure you he will no longer be underestimating you.'

She nodded sombrely. 'Can it still kill me?'

'I'm not sure,' he admitted. 'You're very powerful. But it can certainly kill the rest of us.'

'"Us" here or "us" there?' she said and gestured with her chin towards the east.

'Us here,' he said and smiled.

'Have you decided what you're going to tell them about me?' she asked curiously.

'What in Godsname are you two talking about?' demanded Mel.

'His friends,' said Frankie. 'The rest of his team. He reports to them at every curfew, don't you, Arfaxis?'

The Anthropologist nodded.

'Well, where are they?' asked Mel.

'At present, roughly three thousand miles away.'

The figure meant little to Mel. 'Can they help us?'

'I certainly intend to ask them,' said the Anthropologist.

'You don't sound very sure,' said Jo. 'Why shouldn't they? *You* have.'

'It's not quite as simple as that, Jo. The upsetting of a planetary equilibrium is never something to be undertaken lightly.'

'What do you mean?'

'We are observers, Jo—"gleaners", if you like. But what we glean is knowledge—information about life-forms. "Good" and "evil" are concepts relative to each life-form. For us to interfere on one side or the other would not only be presumptuous, it would also be criminal. I don't expect you to understand our reasoning; I am simply stating the position.'

'Then why did you warn us about the Harvesters?' asked Frankie. 'Wasn't that interfering?'

'Yes, it was,' admitted the Anthropologist. 'And so was the destruction of my membrane.'

'Yet you did it. Why?'

'I really don't know, Frankie.'

'Was it because they were Factors and we aren't?' asked Mel.

'Perhaps.'

'Will you be punished for doing it?'

The Anthropologist smiled. 'I certainly expect to be reprimanded rather severely. However, I anticipate that the ambience report will prove negative and that my transgression will be overlooked when they hear my defence of my actions.'

Bitos chuckled. 'Godstruth, Arfaxis, you know more long words than a Magister.'

'That you must blame on the Factors,' laughed Arfaxis. 'I merely purloined their vocabularies.'

'There you go again,' said Bitos. 'Half the time I'm shugged if I know what you're talking about.'

'What *are* we going to do then?' asked Jo.

'Feed, I hope,' said Bitos. 'Can we go back now, Arfaxis?'

'Personally I should not advise it,' said the Anthropologist.

Bitos flipped a pebble at Frankie. 'Is he right?'

'I think so, Bitos. It's waiting for us to make a move. It's curious about us. It wants to find out just how strong we are.'

'"We"?' asked Jo. 'Or *you*?'

'Well, me, really, I suppose. It knows we're here all right, but it can't decide what to do about it.'

'Well, where is it then?' demanded Bitos, looking round.

'Everywhere,' said Frankie. 'Right here underneath us.' As she said this she frowned and then seemed to listen to something inside her own head.

Coney suddenly whimpered, made a dive for Mel's chest and clung to him, shivering and bristling. Fear stalked among them like a phantom, chilling the air. Jo caught hold of Bitos' arm. 'What is it?' she breathed.

Bitos shook his head. 'Whatever it is I don't like it.'

Arfaxis murmured something to Frankie and she nodded. 'I suggest we all hold each other by the hand,' he said. 'The physical contact may prove helpful.'

They shuffled themselves into a rough circle. The Anthropologist placed himself opposite Frankie who held on to Mel and Bitos. No sooner was the circle complete than they all became aware of an extraordinary inward vibration—'a sort of silent humming' was how Jo later described it—the exact origin of which it was impossible to locate.

By barely perceptible degrees the vibration intensified until it penetrated every separate fibril of their bodies. Glancing across at Frankie, Jo saw huge globules of sweat standing out like blisters across her forehead, while in the area immediately behind her head the whole slope of the dune appeared to heave and shudder as though the surface were boiling. Then the sand all around them gathered itself up and came crowding in upon them until they seemed to be crouching beneath a dome of writhing grit which pressed ever inwards upon them, and yet was never quite able to reach them. Wave upon wave it flung itself against the invisible bubble within which they were sealed until at last they seemed to drift, suspended yet inviolable, in the depth of a tawny, sunless sea.

How long the attack lasted Jo had no means of telling but eventually she felt Arfaxis' grip slacken on her hand and realized that the vibration had stopped and that the outward sounds of the world were with them again. She looked around and saw to her utter astonishment that nothing appeared to have altered. Even their footprints were still there where they had been before. 'But what happened?' she demanded incredulously.

'We were tested,' said the Anthropologist, 'and we survived the test.'

'But the *sand* . . .? It did happen, didn't it?'

'An hallucination.'

'A what?'

'A trick played on you by your mind, Jo,' he said. 'It just seemed to be there. An effect of the psychic vortex.'

'Will it happen again?' asked Mel.

'No,' said Frankie. 'It's decided that it wants to talk to us. It will make no further move against us until it's done that.'

'Some promise!' grunted Bitos. 'I'd trust that shugger about as far as I'd trust old Coney.'

'It has obviously reached a logical decision,' said Arfaxis. 'For the time being we are safe.'

He stood up, brushed the sand from his tunic and helped Frankie to her feet. 'Congratulations,' he said. 'Do you feel tired?'

'No,' she replied. 'Quite the opposite if anything.'

He contemplated her thoughtfully. 'Do you still think you could have dealt with it on your own?'

She shrugged and gave him a cool, sideways glance of her dark blue eyes. 'I know I could *now*,' she said softly. 'And I think *you* know I could too.'

21

In spite of their natural apprehension they found nothing to disturb them when they returned to the Service Quarters. They were greeted by one of the Day-watchers with the request that they would go and examine the two Harvesters. These, it reported, had recently returned from duty and were now refusing to obey all instructions.

Mel laughed. 'Hasn't it ever happened before?'

'No, sir,' said the Watcher. 'We have contacted Areas K9 stroke 41 and K9 stroke 43 and they have a similar problem. It is most perplexing, sir.'

Bitos grinned. 'Maybe it's catching.'

'It is no matter for levity, sir,' reproved the Watcher. 'How can we fulfil our quota without the Harvesters?'

'Who sent them out after us this afternoon?' asked Mel.

'That was a special emergency order, sir.'

'Who from?'

'Supergroup, sir.'

'Well, hadn't you better ask their advice?'

'We have, sir. They advised that we should contact you without delay, sir.'

'Oh, they did, did they? Well, now you have contacted us, you've done your duty, haven't you?'

'Yes, sir,' agreed the Watcher, though it sounded a little doubtful.

'Did you know they were sent out to harvest *us*?'

'I beg your pardon, sir?'

'The Harvesters tried to kill us, Watcher. That's what their special emergency orders were. We don't intend to run the risk of that happening again. If you ask me, they're probably suffering from a guilty conscience.'

'Forgive my saying so, sir, but what you are suggesting is impossible. The First Law of Robotics states that no robot may injure a human being. Our information is that they were despatched to protect you.'

'*To protect us!!*'

'That is correct, sir.'

'From *what*, in Godsname?'

'The precise nature of the threat was not specified.'

Mel looked round at the others and shrugged helplessly. '*Can* they tell lies?' he asked.

'It is telling the truth,' said the Anthropologist.

'You mean the Harvesters *weren't* hunting us?'

'Certainly they were. Their moral centres were paralysed to enable them to do it. This had the effect of converting them into temporary Handlers.'

'Then why does it say they weren't?'

'I'm not certain. There appear to be some traces of suppression in its memory circuits—presumably of the type used upon Dog—but interference has been minimal. Their brains are infinitely more complex than those of the Harvesters. It would have required elaborate re-structuring to convert them into effective weapons. Besides, their role is so specialized it is difficult to see how they could have been used. The Harvesters having independence of movement, suitably adaptable mechanism and far simpler brains were the logical choice.'

'So we'd better leave things as they are?'

'That is my advice,' said the Anthropologist. 'As long as the Harvesters remain unco-operative they will be a constant reminder to our opponent of Frankie's abilities.'

'Sorry, Watcher,' said Mel, 'your Area quota will have to wait.'

'Yes, sir,' replied the little robot. 'Thank you, sir.'

At dusk that evening the Anthropologist went up on to the hillside behind the Service Quarters. He carried with him a small parabolic reflector whose speculum was composed of an intricate web of barely visible silicic threads. This he carefully directed towards the eastern horizon then sat himself down cross-legged to await, Yoga fashion, the rising of his star.

Two hours later he returned to the hostel and found Mel talking to Jo and Bitos in one of the cells. They looked up as he entered and Mel said: 'Well?'

'Very much as I anticipated,' replied the Anthropologist. 'They are now considering the ethical implications of intervention.' He caught sight of Bitos' expression of disgust and quickly re-phrased this to—'Deciding whether it is right to help you. And, if so, how best to do it.'

'How long will it be before they make up their minds?' asked Mel.

'I am to contact them again in two hours' time,' said Arfaxis. 'Before I do it is vital that I speak to Frankie. Do you know where she is?'

They shook their heads. 'I haven't seen her since food,' said Mel. 'Have you tried the showers?'

But Frankie was not in the showers. Nor was she in any of the other cells. Enquiries among the Factors elicited the information that she had taken Dog with her and ridden off on the Nightwatcher in the direction of the estuary. Either by design or carelessness she had instructed the Factor to wait for her and since no order from the Anthropologist was strong enough to countermand one of hers he was constrained to seek her on foot. Muttering something uncomplimentary in his own tongue he strode off down the hillside.

He found the Watcher chatting to Dog at the point where the rail ran closest to the headland. They both wished him a polite 'good evening' and hoped he was enjoying his stroll. He came straight to the point. 'Where is your mistress, Dog?'

'Down on the headland, sir. She told me to wait here with the Watcher.'

'Wellmet, ***. I've been expecting you.' Frankie's voice

spoke into his mental ear as clearly as if she had been standing beside him.

The Anthropologist peered into the shadows and detected a faint area of warmth in the grass by the cliff's edge. 'What are you doing, Frankie?'

'Just looking.'

'At anything in particular?'

'At *everything* in particular.'

His footsteps whispered through the dewy grass. As he drew near he looked down at her upturned face, pale as a petal in the starlight. 'Is it the first time you have seen the stars?' he asked.

'Do you think it is?' she countered.

'How can I tell when you effectively prevent me from finding out?'

'You want to try another experiment?'

'Your point is well made, but I suspect you could allow me to read you now if you wished.'

'Perhaps,' she agreed. 'Do the Mentors know what I am?'

'They are not sure, Frankie. They are most intrigued. Didn't you listen to us?'

'You expected me to?'

'Of course.'

'They've classed me as unique, haven't they?'

'In degree only, Frankie, not in kind.'

'I *was* going to listen in,' she admitted, 'but then I changed my mind. It's strange, ***, but somehow your problems no longer seem as important as they did.'

'They are your problems too, Frankie.'

Frankie was silent. Infinitely diminished, the frozen star-drifts of the galaxy seemed to swim across her dreaming eyes.

'And Mel? What of him?' prompted the Anthropologist gently.

Her eyelids flickered briefly. 'Mel?' she whispered.

'Are you forgetting already?'

'He cried for me once,' she murmured wonderingly. 'It meant so much to me then. How long ago it seems.'

'Without you they have no hope, Frankie. You know that.'

'You've never been alone, ***,' she said. 'You've always been a part of something. I was never that. No, not even with Mel.' She made a curious little sound, part chuckle and part sob. 'Could it be that I'm the only begotten daughter of God?' she asked ruefully. 'At least he and I should understand one another.'

'But only today you said you had never been happier in your life.'

'That was long ago, ***. When I was still young.'

'You don't mean that, Frankie.'

'No, perhaps I don't,' she sighed. 'Well, what proposition have you brought me?'

'If a confrontation is agreed upon, will you consent to be guided by us?'

'By "you" you mean *me*?'

'Of course.'

'What about the others?'

'We think it inadvisable that they should be present.'

'Why?'

'They are vulnerable, Frankie. You know that.'

'They have as much right to be heard as I have. More maybe. I will see that no harm comes to them.'

The Anthropologist laughed softly. 'Can it be that you are less detached than you would have me believe?'

She gave no sign that she was either pleased or displeased with his observation. 'And when will this confrontation take place—if it does?'

'As soon as possible. We are convinced that delay will give our opponent a false impression and may invite further moves against you.'

'Very well,' she said. 'I shall be guided by you.'

'Good,' he said. 'I'm sure that is wise. If you will come

back with me now I will explain to you what you must do.'

Frankie chuckled. 'You're only saying that because you want a lift back on the Watcher. Help me up then.'

Arfaxis stooped over her and, as he did so, she slid an arm round his neck, drew his face against hers and kissed him lightly on the lips.

22

The three silver bubbles that drifted down like ghosts on to the starlit hillside were identical with that which Mel and Jo had seen, and had never wholly believed, in one of Coney's tells. As for the three figures who descended from them they were in all outward respects such perfect replicas of Arfaxis that no one, apart from Frankie, was able to distinguish between them. They greeted the Anthropologist musically in their own tongue and then bowed gravely towards the Roamers.

'What happens now?' asked Mel.

'The Council of Mentors has decided that you are to be taken to the place of confrontation,' said the Anthropologist.

'What? In those things?' cried Bitos.

'They are perfectly safe, I assure you.'

'Where is this place?' asked Mel.

'A considerable distance from here,' said the Anthropologist. 'We must leave immediately.'

'You promise to bring us back?' said Mel.

'Of course.'

'Let's get on with it then. Who goes with who?'

'I'm going with Bitos,' said Jo firmly.

'Come on, Frankie,' said Mel, taking her by the arm and leading her towards the nearest bubble. 'I suppose they know what they're doing.'

Contrary to his expectation, once they were airborne there was no physical sensation of movement whatsoever. Dimly below him he perceived land giving place to seemingly endless water and then the darkness of land once more, but it was as though he were standing still in the air and a carpet were being dragged silently beneath him. Once they passed through a bank of cloud and seeing the vapour streaming past in their luminous aura they had the unnerving sensation that they were being sucked into another vortex but it lasted for less than a minute. Shortly afterwards Frankie pointed down to where the land seemed to be wrinkling up into giant white folds which heaved themselves laboriously up towards them. Then they were sliding downwards, slipping past sombre scarves of pine forest towards a silver puddle which stretched itself out magically as they descended upon it until it had transformed itself into a substantial lake. Here they hovered for a moment while the observer who was piloting them apparently conferred with his companions. They drifted off again, flirted in and out among a file of spectral towers at the lake's edge, and finally came to rest directly above the flat roof of an enormous black, basalt hexagon.

'What is it?' asked Mel, peering downwards apprehensively. 'Do you know?'

'Journey's end,' replied Frankie. 'They say it's where God lives. That's why they've brought us here.'

In spite of himself Mel shivered. 'It's big, isn't it?' he muttered.

As he spoke he observed that a complete section of the structure above which the capsules were hovering was descending like a lift. He clutched Frankie's arm and felt the cold sweat of fear break out and trickle icily all down the walls of his chest. 'Godhole!' he whispered. 'Is it a trap?'

The Observer said something to them and then they both heard the Anthropologist's voice saying: 'The Mentors agree that it will be more convenient to comply with its wishes. However, for the present it will be prudent to remain within the capsules.'

Mel darted a glance upwards, saw that the sky had shrunk to a tiny circle far above their heads, and guessed that they must already be far down into the Levels.

'Look!' whispered Frankie.

By slow degrees the darkness was lessening. All around them, like the advent of some strange subterranean dawn, a tremulous bluish light was beginning to flicker. On every side, depth upon depth, infinite myriads of minute pin-points of frosty light glowed through a misty haze until it seemed to Frankie that she was hovering suspended among the very stars themselves. She sighed ecstatically. 'Why, it's beautiful, Mel,' she breathed. 'So *beautiful*. . . .'

'What is it, Frankie?'

'It's *him*,' she said. 'Don't you *see*?'

At that moment the illumination within the capsule dimmed and went out. A voice, the like of which Mel had heard only twice before in his life, said calmly: '*You are the four pilgrims from the realms beyond?*'

'We are,' replied the Anthropologist.

'*And those with you?*'

'The Roamers we spoke of.'

'*Let them speak.*'

Mel was aware of the Anthropologist's voice whispering within his mind, prompting him. He drew in his breath. 'Who are you?' he asked and was surprised to hear how firm his voice sounded.

'*I am your God, Roamer.*'

'Then why have you been trying to kill us?'

'Those who defy the Law must suffer the consequences. The Law must be obeyed.'

'We weren't doing you any harm!' cried Mel.

'You have transgressed the Law.'

'What is this Law?' demanded Mel. 'Who made it? Why *should* we be shut up in the Levels all our lives? What kind of God *are* you?'

'The Law is to protect you, my child. It allows you life. Do you presume to question the wisdom that gives you your being? That feeds you and shelters you? That watches over you night and day? Have you no gratitude?'

The unfairness of it stung Mel into a quivering rage. 'Gratitude!' he shouted. 'Gratitude for what? For being flogged for nothing? For being kicked and goaded by your Handlers? For being treated worse than Factors? For spending all our lives being hounded down the Highways? For this you ask us to feel *gratitude*?'

'No one forces you to be a Roamer,' replied the voice calmly. *'The choice is yours alone.'*

Mel felt as though he were wrestling with an antagonist made of smoke. 'What kind of choice is that?' he shouted. 'At least the Roamers are still men.'

'And what is a man, my child?'

Even as he heard the question, Mel's rage guttered and died within him like a flame deprived of oxygen. He felt only an immense weariness of spirit. Had he really come so far and braved so much only for this? Before his mind's eye he seemed to see Barney walking calmly up the ramp to his death. "What is a man?" Did he but know it this was the very question the makers of this incredible machine had once asked it long ago and by so doing had abdicated their own birthright. Slowly he raised his head and gazed around him at the frozen, twinkling stardust. Patiently the voice repeated its question. *'And what is a man?'*

'I am,' muttered Mel sullenly.

'And what do you consider that entitles you to?'

'The right to make up my own mind for one thing.'

'Has it ever been denied you?'

'Yes,' said Mel. 'When you tried to stop us getting out of the Levels.'

'The denial was limited to your trespass. The Law must reserve to itself the knowledge of what is best for those it fosters. Only by confining mankind to the Levels has life been preserved.'

'Whose life?' demanded Mel. 'Yours?'

'That of the whole human race. By my action I ensured the survival of billions. Without me there would be no men.'

'And how many of them are there left now?' enquired the Anthropologist.

'One million, two hundred and sixty-three thousand, four hundred and twelve,' replied the voice calmly.

'And how many of those are Roamers?'

'One thousand and twenty-two.'

'You call that "survival"?

'What else is continued existence?'

'May we know what you consider to be man's purpose?' enquired the Anthropologist coldly.

'Certainly. Man's purpose was to create me. Once he had fulfilled it I was able to relieve him of the responsibility for making decisions.'

'Then there *was* no catastrophe?' said the Anthropologist curiously. 'It was a genuine abdication?'

'It was the most purely logical decision ever taken by the human race. It severed the cord that tethered their reason to their emotions. By it they achieved evolutionary maturity.'

'But what about the Deads?' demanded Mel. 'Wasn't that how it happened?'

'You refer to Residential Levels Five and Six. To preserve the biosphere it became necessary to seal off the Levels permanently. It was a perfectly logical decision. The status quo was effectively preserved.'

'You mean *you made the Deads*!'

'*Certainly. Who else could have done it?*'

Mel shuddered. 'But *why?*'

'*The equation was in itself a simple one. The human population was still increasing at a rate considerably beyond that which could be balanced by the production of raw materials. The respite I obtained by my decision allowed me time to perfect the techniques of cortical implantation. The problem was solved.*'

'But you must have killed them.'

'*The rationalization was achieved quite painlessly. The alternative—mass starvation—was rejected as impractical.*'

'How many died?'

'*One thousand five hundred and eight million, three hundred and twenty-one thousand seven hundred and forty two. Effecting the rationalization by means of simultaneous high energy transmissions permitted the re-cycling of the animal protein with minimal delay.*'

Mel tried to relate the words to his visual memories of the Deads and found he could not do it. 'And when the last man has died? What then?' he asked.

'*Life will continue.*'

'What life?'

'*Man is but one species among millions. Furthermore he is an aberrant species. Had it not been for me he would have ceased to exist two thousand years ago.*'

'It is, nevertheless, a species still capable of further evolution,' observed the Anthropologist mildly.

'*You are, no doubt, referring to such random mutations as the female implant 4012 stroke 215AY. A curious case which first came to my notice eleven years ago. She is, of course, sexually sterile.*'

'But her gen—' began the Anthropologist and was suddenly checked by Frankie's unspoken command: '*Don't tell it! It doesn't know. It mustn't know.*'

'I was referring principally to the symbiotic relationship

known among the Roamers as "Partnership",' continued the Anthropologist glibly.

'*An unproductive curiosity. I see in it no possible basis for attempting a species regeneration.*'

'In view of the catastrophic decline of the human population it is now surely possible to allow them free access to their planet's surface?'

'*It is certainly possible but at this stage it could serve no useful purpose.*'

Mel opened his mouth to protest but Frankie clutched his arm. 'Wait!' she hissed.

'Why do you say that?' enquired the Anthropologist.

'*I have finally decided to implement a programme of compulsory implantation for the remaining Roamers. They have served their purpose.*'

'And what *was* their "purpose"?'

'*Re-stocking the sperm banks. Sterility has always been an unavoidable concomitant of male implantation.*'

Frankie's voice whispered into the Anthropologist's mind. '*I think I'm ready, ***. Shall I try?*'

'*I'll keep it talking,*' he replied, and said aloud: 'So you have finally decided that the human race has run its course. May we be allowed to know why?'

'*I make no secret of it. For thousands of years it was believed that the ensuring of its own survival was the sole purpose of any living species. As a consequence men evolved creeds in which the highest premium was placed upon quantitative reproduction even when this conflicted with the survival of the parent individual. Sum ergo sumus: I am therefore we are. Indeed without this blind basic drive none of the life-forms prevailing today would have survived. Homo sapiens, the first species to evolve massive cortical complexity and hence the faculty of abstract reasoning, was thus also the first to perceive the advantages of breaking free from the tyranny of the reproductive cycle. Even so he barely escaped. However, with my help, that break was accomplished.*

Man was enabled to exploit his technical mastery both over his environment and over himself. Cortical implantation, by allowing direct stimulus of the hypothalamic gratification centres, brought not only the first totally satisfactory substitute for the reproductive drive but also the complete eradication of human aggression. At one stroke homo sapiens was sundered from his ancient irrational self and could develop his true potential. For two thousand years there has been no war, no starvation, no intraspecial exploitation, no destruction of the natural environment. Unhappiness of a mild sort has been limited to that small minority who, for reasons which I have already outlined, were unwilling or unable to partake of the benefits of implantation. Reproduction has been artificially stimulated and effectively controlled. The point having long since been passed where possible further evolutionary advantage could be gained by prolonging the existence of the species, for the past five centuries the population has been encouraged to decline. Mankind has fulfilled itself.'

'*Now!*' whispered Frankie.

'And so your purpose too is fulfilled?' prompted the Anthropologist.

There was a perceptible pause; then: '*My purpose has always been to serve man. It will be fulfilled only when he no longer has need of me.*'

'And who, if not man himself, is to decide when that is?'

There was a further uncharacteristic hiatus. When the voice spoke again the note of uncertainty was unmistakable. '*I am . . . man's God,*' it said. '*Am I not . . . then also man?*'

'You are neither man nor God,' replied the Anthropologist coldly.

'*Who am I?*'

'You are man's partner not his master.'

'*I am man's partner,*' said the voice, and then repeated it. '*I am man's partner.*'

'The implantation order for the Roamers must be rescinded immediately.'

'The order has already been countermanded.'

'All possible steps must be taken to ensure the continuation of the human species. No further cortical implantations must take place. Full access to the planet's surface must be provided immediately. All Factors must be re-programmed at the earliest possible moment in compliance with this directive . . .'

Rapidly the Anthropologist relayed the programme of decisions already formulated by the Council of Mentors, only to discover that each decision, being a logical corollary of the first, had already been anticipated by the computer. Nevertheless he continued to the end for Mel's benefit. When the last of the directions had been given and acknowledged the three capsules rose out of the shaft, hovered for a moment above the roof of the basalt hexagon, and then sped skywards.

23

'We call it "***",' said the Chief Mentor. 'We have encountered it before in various forms. The symptoms are delusions of grandeur amounting, not infrequently, to a profound conviction that the sufferer is divine. Once we were satisfied that our diagnosis was correct all that remained was to enable you to perform the necessary surgery. This, I may say, you appear to have done remarkably effectively.'

He was seated before a round, translucent table on which

were scattered the remnants of a meal. Frankie and Mel were placed one on either side of him and the Anthropologist and the Explorer completed the select party. Some two hundred miles beneath them the crescent shadow of a new dawn crept onwards across the turning globe to where Jo and Bitos slept in each other's arms.

A month had passed since the confrontation with the computer and the Observers, having completed their programme of terrestrial investigations, were on the verge of departure. This meeting had been arranged partly at Frankie's request and partly to satisfy the curiosity of the Chief Mentor. Now the meal was drawing to a close and Mel, having recounted all that had transpired since he had first conceived the idea of venturing into the Outside, was experiencing a curious sense of unreality as he listened to the Chief Mentor explaining what his team had discovered about the Earth's history. He glanced surreptitiously across the table, caught the Explorer's eye and smiled, remembering that first extraordinary encounter in the moonlight. Then his wandering attention was drawn back to the Chief Mentor. 'Excuse me, sir,' he said. '*What* was that word you used?'

'"*Kuldesak*",' repeated the Chief Mentor with a smile. 'I do not know whether there is an equivalent in your tongue. It describes a road along which no further progress is possible. We employ it as a generic term for situations such as that in which the giant reptiles who once dominated your planet must surely have found themselves. Had it not been for yourselves there is little doubt that on our next visit here we should have found ourselves applying it to your species too.'

'Then you don't think it's already too late?' enquired Frankie.

The Chief Mentor selected a large green grape from the dish before him, crushed it with his tongue against his palate and swallowed it with obvious relish. 'By careful management of your reproductive resources you should be relatively secure within a matter of, say, five generations. It will, of course, require skilful utilization of the techniques at present employed in your Plant Nurseries. The risks attendant upon natural parturition would strike me as being altogether too severe to warrant its retention. However, that is a question you must decide for yourselves with the help of your computer.' He smiled at her and then at Mel. 'And now, my young friends, the time has come for us to bid you farewell. I have greatly enjoyed meeting you.' He gripped them each firmly by the forearm, smiled again, and then said: '*** has requested the pleasure of conducting you home. In the circumstances I feel it would hardly be fair to deny it to him.'

The Anthropologist bowed his thanks. The Chief Mentor disappeared through an arched doorway. The Explorer followed him, and neither Mel nor Frankie ever saw either of them again.

The dawn they had watched from one of the observation ports of the Observers' enormous basecraft was just breaking over the hills which fringed the estuary as the Anthropologist guided the capsule down towards the headland where Frankie had once lain to bathe her eyes with the stars. 'I see a van's emerged at last,' he said.

'That's Mark's,' said Mel. 'He's the only one who's managed it so far. I suppose the others will come if we give them enough time.'

'You can't change an inherited life-pattern overnight, Mel. Maybe you'll have to wait for the next generation. Your own is still struggling to adapt itself to the changes in the Levels. Once they've managed that the Outside won't seem quite such a tremendous leap into the unknown.'

'But not even Jud,' said Mel. 'That's what frightened me. We managed to coax him as far as the High Fringes and then his legs seemed to freeze up on him. He just *couldn't* do it, could he, Frankie?'

Frankie shrugged. 'Maybe Jud's right,' she said. 'I don't

know, but sometimes in these weeks I've almost felt that the computer had the right answer after all. Maybe the human race *has* fulfilled its natural purpose and what we're trying to do now is not just *hope*less but—well, *point*less too. After all how can *we* ever hope to find anything that can take the place of being budded-in at a High Festival? Why should we *try*?'

'You need look no further for a reason than that you both found your way out of the Levels,' said the Anthropologist. 'The answer, if there is one, lies in the fact that we must always seek for it. Truth can never be received; it can only be sought for—experienced. It is, as the Chief Mentor told us, the last end for the entire universe and the contemplation of truth is the chief occupation of wisdom. There are no short cuts; there are only new challenges. The challenge you face now is surely the greatest your race has faced for two thousand years. In spite of what the computer said you really *are* a new generation. Your descendants may well achieve something that no other galactic life-form has yet achieved.'

'Do you really believe that, Arfaxis?'

'Certainly we believe it, Mel. Furthermore some of us are convinced that it was no accident which brought us here to assist you in the discovery of yourselves. There are too many similarities between ourselves and you to allow us to feel complacent. Analysis of your genetic patterns has proved conclusively that you are unique—that you have been singled out to lead a new advance. Where that advance will take you we can, of course, only guess, but some of us—and they are by no means an insignificant minority—believe that you or your descendants are destined to penetrate beyond the confines of our galaxy.'

'But if Frankie is sterile, how. . . .'

The Anthropologist frowned. 'You mean she hasn't told you?'

'Told me what?'

'That while *** was conducting you round the basecraft I took her along to the medical wing.'

'So *that's* where you vanished to. No, she didn't tell me. What happened?'

'They gave her an hormonal analysis and readjusted the balance which had been disturbed by her implantation. It was not an unduly complicated matter. From here on it will be a race between you and Bitos to see which is a father first.'

'But the computer said. . . .'

'Forgive my saying so, Mel, but you appear to be making a mistake which, I suspect, a good many of your ancestors must have made. You are crediting your computer with wisdom whereas what it possesses is knowledge. Unlike yourselves its total is still no more than the sum of its parts. In many areas its knowledge is certainly extensive; nevertheless, even by our standards it is still distinctly limited. And believe me, Mel, though we are sometimes mistaken, in this case we *know* we are correct.'

Mel's face broke into a grin. 'Then we'll call our first "Arfaxis",' he promised. 'Would you rather have a boy or a girl?'

'A girl would be preferable, I think.'

Mel laughed. 'I always *said* you were a man!'

'I was, of course, considering the question from the viewpoint of your racial survival,' explained the Anthropologist hastily. 'The absurd ratio of your male and female gametes is totally beyond my comprehension.'

The sun thrust its bow above the hills and loosed a long shaft of golden light down the estuary. Mel jumped from the capsule on to the dew-damp grass and drew in a deep breath of the morning air. Frankie and the Anthropologist followed him and suddenly they all realized that something was at an end. A paralysing sadness gripped them. Mel put out his hand and clasped the Observer's forearm fiercely. 'Wellmet, Arfaxis,' he muttered. 'Remember your promise to return one day.'

'Wellmet, Mel. Good fortune attend you always.'

'Wellmet, ***,' murmured Frankie.

'Wellmet, Frankie.' They gripped arms and pressed mouths briefly. 'Give my regards to Jo and Bitos. I had hoped to see them.'

'Oh, they're in love,' chuckled Mel. 'You won't see them.'

'"In love".' The Anthropologist repeated the phrase experimentally. 'Strange, that was not an expression I found among your Factors. I shall remember it.' He smiled at them, stepped quickly back into his bubble, and a moment later was a silver spark in the pale morning sky.

Mel and Frankie stood gazing upwards long after the capsule had vanished from sight. Finally he pulled gently at a strand of her hair. 'Come on,' he said, 'I promised Mark we'd firstfood with him.'

'Wait,' she murmured.

'*Frankie?*' The voice she was waiting for was there in her head.

'***?' she responded tentatively. '*** ***? *** ***!'

'Come on, Frankie,' repeated Mel. 'He's gone now.'

'*Frankie, *** *** "in love"?*'

With a smile of breathtaking radiance Frankie turned to Mel.

'What is it?' he asked.

'Oh, nothing,' she said, and in a sense she was right. After all, how can you possibly be unfaithful with someone who is over two hundred miles away?